EXCELLER
SELECT

TOP PICKS

No Lotus for
MEERA SINHA

No Lotus for
MEERA SINHA

A Spiritual Thriller on Love and Fate

Chandrashekhar Siva

EXCELLER BOOKS®
A GLOBAL PRESS

No Lotus for Meera Sinha
A Spiritual Thriller on Love and Fate

Cover by Exceller Books

ISBN: 978-93-47397-59-2

Published in India in 2025 by Exceller Books,
An imprint of GE Group,
G1, Dream Apartment, Degree College Road, Belgharia,
Kolkata, 700056, India
www.excellerbooks.com

EXCELLER BOOKS®
A GLOBAL PRESS

Dedication

To **Priya**—
my wife, my first love, and the soul of every journey I take.
Your faith in me is the light I walk by.

To **Smita**—
my daughter, my joy, and my inspiration.
You remind me every day why stories must be told with heart.

सत्यं वद, धर्मं चर
Satyam vada, dharmam chara
"Speak the truth, walk the path of righteousness."

May this story walk with truth and dharma,
and may it forever carry the fragrance of the love and grace you both bring into my life.

Acknowledgements

This book has been a journey of many hearts and hands, and I am deeply grateful to those who stood beside me through it all.

First and foremost, my deepest love and gratitude to my wife, Priya, whose quiet strength and unwavering support have been the foundation of my creative journey. And to my daughter, Smita, the joy of my life, whose innocent laughter reminds me each day of life's purest truths.

To the editors, reviewers, and publishing professionals — thank you for believing in the story of Meera Sinha. Your guidance and encouragement have helped shape this book into what it is today.

I also wish to acknowledge Vedanta Kesari, where my children's stories are being welcomed for publication. It is an honour to be part of a legacy that inspires young minds through the lens of Sanatana Dharma.

Lastly, I am grateful for the quiet moments, the midnight musings, and the inner voice that kept whispering, "Keep writing. She's waiting to be heard."

Foreword

Some stories arrive not with thunder, but like the soft rustle of leaves—quiet, persistent, and deeply rooted in truth. *No Lotus for Meera Sinha* is one such tale. It doesn't scream for attention; it unfolds gently, layer by layer, revealing a woman's soul caught between duty and desire, silence and survival, shadows and awakening.

Set against the backdrop of modern India yet echoing ancient truths, this novel is more than a suspense thriller. It is a reflection of Sanatana Dharma—the timeless wisdom of dharma, karma, inner struggle, and the transformative power of grace. It is about choices, consequences, and the silence that speaks louder than words.

In Meera's world, the lotus does not bloom in clear waters. Her truth emerges from mud, pain, and uncertainty. Yet, like the sacred flower, her journey, too, is a search for meaning, for clarity, for redemption.

This book is not written merely to entertain. It is written to stir, to linger, to awaken questions in the quiet corners of the reader's heart. Let the story begin not just on these pages, but within you.

– Sripriya Sundararaman Siva
Author
Umachi Books

Preface

This story was not born in a moment. It took shape slowly, quietly—like a seed waiting for the right season to sprout. *No Lotus for Meera Sinha* emerged from the many silences I've lived with, the stories I've observed but could never tell out loud, and the emotions I've carried deep within me.

The idea came with a question: What does it mean to live a life that is externally calm but internally stormy? Meera Sinha, the protagonist, came to me as an answer. She represents the many women—and men—who live restrained lives, yet burn with questions, ache with longing, and carry unspoken truths in their hearts.

Though inspired by the atmosphere and tone of certain noir classics, this book stands on its own—steeped in Indian soil, wrapped in the spiritual depth of Sanatana Dharma, and shaped by the emotional rhythms of everyday life. It is not a retelling; it is a remembering, a story that honours both shadow and light.

In writing this, I did not chase perfection. I chased honesty. I wrote to understand, to heal, and to grow.

If this book makes you pause, reflect, or feel something quietly stirring within, then it has done what it was meant to do.

With deep gratitude,
Chandrashekhar Siva

Author's Note

No Lotus for Meera Sinha is a work of fiction. But like all stories, it draws breath from the world around us—from the quiet despair behind closed doors, from the strength hidden in fragile hearts, from the enduring spirit of those who never lose hope, even when everything else is lost.

While this novel is rooted in Indian culture and layered with the quiet undercurrents of Sanatana Dharma, it is not religious in tone. Instead, it is spiritual—about human struggle, karmic consequences, choices made in silence, and the price of truth. There is no preaching here, only storytelling.

I have done my best to keep the characters honest, the narrative engaging, and the emotions real. Though inspired in tone by noir classics, particularly *No Orchids for Miss Blandish*, this book is entirely my own—set in a world I know, shaped by the values I hold, and written with complete originality. Any resemblance to real persons or events is purely coincidental.

This book is dedicated to the two greatest loves of my life—my wife, Priya, and my daughter, Smita. Without their presence, this story—and perhaps even the storyteller—would not exist.

I thank you, dear reader, for walking this path with Meera. You may not always agree with her choices, but I hope you will understand the depth of her journey.

— *Chandrashekhar Siva*

Table of Contents

Part 1
The Abduction

Chapter 1

The Letter in the Courtyard

The Silence between Footsteps

The courtyard smelled of wet earth and burnt jasmine. Meera stood barefoot under the neem tree, the gravel cool beneath her feet, her white cotton saree soaked with rain at the edges. The morning had begun like any other in her ancestral haveli in Varanasi — the conch blowing at dawn, the temple bells echoing from the ghat, and the scent of filter coffee rising from the kitchen. But the letter in her hand changed everything.

It had no sender's name. Only her name — *Meera Sinha* — was written in an unfamiliar hand, sharp and deliberate. The envelope was ivory-colored, the kind used decades ago. Inside, on thick parchment, only a single line was written: *"The lotus never blooms twice. Come to where the river bends."*

After reading it three times, she began reading it a fourth time, tracing each word with trembling fingers. She was not new to riddles — her father had raised her with ancient puzzles and tales of sages who spoke in symbols — but this felt different. It was not poetic. It was a warning.

Behind her, the rustle of slippers on stone broke her trance. Lakshmi, the old housekeeper, approached with concern.

"*Beti*, breakfast is ready. Should I bring it to your room?"

Meera folded the letter quickly and slipped it into her blouse. "No, Lakshmi amma. I'll come inside soon."

Lakshmi hesitated. "You're standing in the rain again. You'll catch a cold."

"I like the rain," Meera replied with a soft smile. "It washes off what shouldn't stay."

As the old woman retreated, Meera looked at the neem tree above her — the same tree where her mother used to hang marigold garlands, the same one where a pair of owls nested every *Kartik* month. Childhood memories flickered in her mind — the secret games with her brother Arjun, the stolen laddoos, and the stories whispered at dusk. But those days were long gone. Arjun had vanished three years ago. Some said he ran away. Some said he drowned.

And now this letter.

She returned to her room, opened the ancient teak almirah, and retrieved a diary bound in black leather — her father's. Inside were notes, diagrams, and references to Vedic texts. She flipped to a page he had marked with a lotus symbol. There it was — a reference to the *Bhrigu Samhita*, and an annotation: *"Where the river bends — time folds."*

Her breath caught. Her father always spoke in metaphors. But if this letter was connected to the secrets he had once hinted at — forbidden knowledge, lost rituals, karmic debts — then she couldn't ignore it.

That night, as thunder growled and the Ganga whispered against the stone ghats, Meera packed a small satchel with a journal, her father's copper ring, a photograph of Arjun, and a folded white dupatta that smelled faintly of sandalwood.

She left a note on her writing desk: *"I'm going to find the truth. Don't follow me."*

Then she stepped out, into the night, not knowing that the moment she crossed the iron gates of the *haveli*, someone had already begun following her — a shadow cloaked in silence, with eyes that did not blink.

Shadows of the Banyan

The sun had begun to retreat behind the mango grove as Meera sat cross-legged in the inner courtyard, her eyes fixed on the banyan tree whose roots curled like aged fingers into the earth. The letter still lay unopened beside her, its envelope slightly creased from the trembling of her hands earlier.

A parrot shrieked somewhere above, shaking loose a flurry of dry leaves. Meera's gaze rose. That tree—her late father used to say it had stood since the time of Shivaji. Its gnarled trunk had witnessed wars, weddings, and even whispers of betrayal. And now, it stood witness to *her* moment of hesitation.

Meera was not a woman easily shaken. Thirty-four, quiet but firm, she was known in her village of Pahadpur for running the small primary school with care and discipline. But the envelope's presence had unsettled her like no government order or corrupt official's visit ever had.

It had come that morning—unstamped, hand-delivered. Radha, the house help, had found it tucked beneath the brass bell by the tulsi altar. There was no name, no sign—just a plain envelope sealed with a thin strip of turmeric-yellow thread.

Meera reached for it now and held it close to her heart for a breath. Her instincts whispered this letter was not ordinary.

She turned the envelope in her fingers. The paper was thick, like something out of a different time. She could still faintly smell sandalwood on it.

She remembered her mother used to write letters like this—pressed with jasmine petals, tied with thread, always starting with: *"To the one who carries light."*

The memory stung like a warm breeze turning cold too fast. She tore the envelope carefully.

Inside was a single sheet. It was folded thrice and blank on the outside. Her heart started thudding in her ears as she unfolded it slowly.

The ink was a deep blue, almost black. The letters curved as if they had been drawn rather than written. She read the words once, then twice. Her hands began to tremble again.

"What you seek is not lost, Meera.

But it must not be found too soon. The past was buried for a reason. But the lotus knows where to bloom again. Midnight. Temple steps. Come alone."

She sat motionless for several minutes. Even the breeze seemed to hold its breath. No name, no signature—only a familiar, ghostly knowing in the words.

Who knew about the lotus? About *that* past?

Her fingers curled around the letter. She looked up at the banyan tree again. A single yellow leaf fluttered down and landed at her feet, like an omen—or a promise.

She stood up slowly. Her world had just shifted again.

Shadows in the Paper

Meera stared at the letter for a long time sitting at the courtyard, the harsh creases of the folded envelope etched into her palm. Her heart beat unnaturally loud, thudding in her chest like a drum being played far too close to the ear. Who would send her something with no name, no sender's mark—just those nine chilling words?

"Don't go to the temple. You are being watched."

She slid the letter into her diary, closed it slowly, and walked back inside. The floor tiles felt colder than usual, as if the house itself sensed something was amiss. Her mother was busy rolling out chapatis in the kitchen, humming a soft bhajan, unaware of the unease wrapping itself around her daughter.

Meera didn't mention the letter. Not yet.

Instead, she walked up to her room and locked the door. The room was a haven of calm—walls painted pale lavender, a brass Ganesha idol on the shelf, and rows of books stacked in perfectly measured chaos. But today, even the familiar comfort of her sanctuary couldn't still her thoughts.

She pulled the letter out again and stared at the handwriting. It was slanted, hurried, and oddly precise—almost as if someone who didn't usually write in Hindi had taken the time to do so this once. She turned the envelope inside out, hoping for a clue, but there was nothing—no postmark, no emblem. Had someone dropped it off themselves?

A chill ran down her spine.

Suddenly, the wind picked up, and the wooden windows rattled lightly. The neem tree outside scraped its dry fingers against the glass. Meera stood up abruptly, walked to the window, and looked out.

The narrow lane below was empty, as always on a hot afternoon in Banaras. But something felt... off. A flash of orange cloth disappeared behind the broken boundary wall. A shadow flicked and vanished like a blink. Her throat tightened.

"Am I imagining this?" she whispered.

Her phone buzzed. It was a message from her college friend, Swati.

Swati: "Still meeting at the temple? 4PM sharp? Bring your notes on Kabir Das!"

Meera hesitated. She started typing, deleted it, and then typed again.

Meera: "Yes, I'll be there."

She put the phone down. The words from the letter replayed in her mind—You are being watched.

That sentence hadn't been a threat. It was a warning. And warnings usually meant someone cared enough to prevent what was coming—or was that part of the trap?

She couldn't tell anymore.

Downstairs, the doorbell rang. Three sharp chimes.

Meera flinched.

She peered down through the stairwell. A boy, no older than fourteen, stood holding a brown parcel in both hands. It was a courier.

She opened the door cautiously.

"Meera Sinha?" the boy asked, eyes not meeting hers.

"Yes."

He handed her the parcel, got her signature on a scuffed touchscreen, and disappeared without another word. There was no scooter, no vehicle nearby, and the street was silent again.

She opened the parcel inside.

Inside was a single book—*The Art of Disappearing* by Manish Shukla. There was no sender's name, no invoice, nothing.

While flipping through the pages, a slip of paper fluttered out and landed at her feet.

She picked it up.

There was written in one sentence: *"You've seen him before, but not with your eyes."*

Her knees nearly buckled.

She backed into the nearest chair, her hand over her mouth. The walls of her room seemed to shrink inward, the purple now too dim, and the air too still.

Somewhere in the city, someone was playing a game.

And she was the first piece being moved.

A Stranger in the Mirror

Evening cast its amber glow across Banaras, dyeing the sky in hues of gold and fire. Meera stood at the bathroom sink, splashing water on her face in an attempt to cool her nerves. The message in the book still echoed through her, ringing louder than temple bells: *"You've seen him before, but not with your eyes."*

What did it even mean?

She looked up into the mirror, expecting to see the familiar oval face, brown eyes flecked with green, the tired dark circles under them. But just for a flicker of a second—so brief she could've blamed the play of light—she thought she saw someone else standing behind her.

She spun around but there was no one.

She grabbed her bag, diary, and the Kabir Das notes, forcing herself to breathe evenly. She had agreed to meet Swati at the Vishwanath temple steps by 4 PM and cancelling it now would invite too many questions she wasn't ready to answer.

Her auto ride from the Lanka crossing to the temple was unusually quiet. The city, usually bursting with cycle bells, flower vendors shouting prices, and the echo of shlokas from loudspeakers, felt hushed. Even the cows seemed subdued.

She reached the temple ghat. As she stepped out of the auto, she scanned the crowd. There were tourists in white caps, *sadhus* smeared in ash, and florists hawking garlands. Everything appeared normal, but her instincts wouldn't calm down.

There was a weight in the air.

She walked slowly, scanning for Swati, but there was no sign of her yet.

She sat down on the steps, adjusting her dupatta nervously. To distract herself, she took out the diary and flipped through it until she reached the letter again. Her fingers trembled slightly as she touched the paper. The more she looked at it, the more she felt like it held layers of meaning she couldn't decode.

Just then, a voice broke her concentration.

"Are you Meera Sinha?"

She turned.

A man stood two steps above her. He was probably in his late twenties, had a whitish complexion, and stubble that looked three days old. He wore a faded blue kurta, with sleeves rolled up. Nothing about him screamed danger—but something felt... deliberate.

"I'm sorry, who are you?" she asked.

He didn't answer immediately. He took out a photo from his wallet and handed it to her.

It was a black-and-white image—blurred slightly, like a still from old CCTV footage.

It was her photo standing in front of a bookstore taken two months ago.

Meera's mouth went dry.

"I didn't know who took this photo," she whispered.

The man nodded. "You were already being followed then. You just didn't know it."

"Who are you?" she asked again, with a harder voice now.

"I can't say yet," he replied. "But you're in danger, Meera. This—this isn't a prank."

Before she could say anything more, a loud horn blared from the road above.

She turned reflexively, and when she turned back, the man was gone.

She scrambled up the steps, looking in every direction, but he'd vanished into thin air, like a whisper swallowed by the city.

And behind her, the photo fluttered to the ground.

Meera picked it up, heart pounding.

On the back, in the same handwriting as the letter, were written three words: *"Trust no one."*

The Silence of Shadows

Night fell upon Varanasi like an ancient silk shawl—soft, dark, and steeped in secrets. The Ganga shimmered under the moonlight, and temple bells began their gentle ringing for the evening *aarti*. Meera sat frozen on the temple steps, the mysterious photograph clutched in her hand. The warning—"*Trust no one*"—looped in her head like a mantra gone wrong.

She had always trusted her instincts. As a literature professor, nuance and subtext were second nature to her. But this? This was no fiction. This was reality.

Her phone buzzed. It was Swati.

Swati: Sorry, Meera! I got caught in traffic. I'm just reaching Lanka. Sorry to make you wait so long.

Meera stared at the message, her thumb hovering over the keyboard. She typed, then deleted. She didn't know what to say. She didn't even know who to trust now. Could she tell Swati?

Instead, she replied:

Meera: Heading home. Not feeling well. Let's talk tomorrow.

She left the *ghat* quickly, avoiding eye contact, her dupatta wrapped tightly around her shoulders like a protective shield. The lanes of old Banaras, which usually offered her a sense of timelessness and comfort, now felt like they were watching her.

She took a longer route back home, bypassing familiar streets. Every time a motorcycle slowed or a stranger lingered too long in her periphery, her heart leapt. She was being followed—of that, she was sure. But by whom?

Reaching home, she bolted the door and drew the curtains tight. Then, she locked herself in her study. She laid the photo and the letter on the desk and stared at them like puzzle pieces from two different games.

She pulled out a thick notebook, usually reserved for student feedback, and began writing:

Day 1: Someone left a letter in my Kabir Das book. There was no signature. It was just a cryptic warning. A man approached me today at Vishwanath Ghat. He knew who I was. He showed me a photo taken months ago, said I was being followed and disappeared before I could question him. The photo has a message: *"Trust no one."* Who is watching me—and why?

She capped the pen and leaned back.

Then, without warning, the power went out.

It was total blackout.

Her apartment sank into complete silence, broken only by the sound of ceiling fans grinding to a halt and distant dogs barking outside. She walked to the window and looked down. The entire lane was dark—no lights in any house. Just the glow of the moon was peering in like a curious visitor.

And then she saw it, a figure, standing across the street under the Gulmohar tree. It was motionless, facing her building. It was not moving, not blinking. It was just there.

Meera's breath caught.

She stepped back, slowly; her heart started thundering.

She had seen that stance before—in a dream, or in a memory she didn't know she possessed.

Chapter 2

The Man Who Knew Her Name

The Stranger in the Mirror

There was always some noise in captivity — a creaking pipe, a distant dog barking, her own heartbeat ricocheting in her ribs. But today, it was unnervingly still, as if the room itself was holding its breath.

She sat on the edge of the cot, arms wrapped tightly around her knees, trying to decipher the change. Something had shifted.

Then came the sound.

It was not the usual clatter of a tray or the soft footfall of the woman in the white sandals. This was heavier and confident. It was the sound of leather soles clicking once, and then pausing, as if waiting to be invited.

Meera stiffened.

The lock turned with an unusual deliberateness. There was no clumsy clanking, just a smooth, practiced twist. The door opened—not wide, just enough for a man to slip through.

He wasn't tall, but he carried himself like someone used to being obeyed. His kurta was neatly pressed, sleeves rolled halfway, revealing forearms that were more scholar than soldier. A watch gleamed at his wrist — gold, antique, and incongruous with the grey room.

But none of that mattered.

What mattered was that he looked straight at her and said, "Meera."

Not "Miss Sinha."

Not "the girl."

Just... Meera.

It wasn't the name alone. It was the way he said it — softly, but with the weight of history, like someone remembering a tune from a childhood lullaby.

She flinched. "Who are you?"

He smiled faintly and pulled a steel chair from the wall, placing it in front of her like a polite interrogator.

"You don't remember me," he said. "But I remember you. Seventeen years ago. St. Thomas Orphanage. Jamshedpur."

Meera's throat went dry. Her mind began scanning dusty corridors of memory, and like a reluctant drawer, one opened and what came out was: a photograph, a visit, and a man with a notebook and a gentle voice, asking her what she wanted to be when she grew up. She had drawn a lotus and said she wanted to become someone who could bloom even in the dirtiest waters.

"You... you were the journalist?"

He nodded. "Ravi Kamat. I was working on a human-interest feature then. You were just twelve then, and your fierce eyes, no one could miss them."

She didn't know what to say. She remembered him now, vaguely, but none of it explained why he was here, or how he knew where she was. She narrowed her eyes.

"Why are you here? What do you want?"

Ravi leaned forward slightly, elbows resting on his knees. "To help. But also, to understand why someone has gone to such great lengths to keep *you* from speaking."

Meera clenched her fists. "You think I know?"

He studied her for a moment, and then exhaled slowly.

"I think you know something. Maybe not consciously. Maybe not in full. But whatever it is, they believe you hold the key. Or the matchstick."

The room felt smaller suddenly.

"I'm not playing these games," she said sharply. "You want to help? Get me out."

"That's not how it works," he replied, his voice calm. "They're watching everything, including this room."

He stood up and walked over to the mirror on the wall — the only ornament in her cell-like world. He tapped it once.

"You ever wonder why they put a mirror in a room with no visitors?"

She stared. The mirror was always there. She had looked into it every day, tracing the tired lines around her eyes, trying to remember her face before fear took it over.

"I thought... maybe it was for me. To remind me I was still human."

He shook his head. "It's a camera, hidden behind the silvered glass, one-way."

Meera swallowed.

Ravi smiled sadly. "You're not just a prisoner here, Meera. You're part of something much bigger. And I'm the last person they'd expect to be helping you."

She looked at him long and hard.

"Why me? Why now?"

He turned to the door but didn't open it. "It is because someone high up has started asking questions. And because I never forgot the girl who drew a lotus in a world of mud."

He walked out before she could say anything.

The door clicked shut again. And this time, the silence felt like a message.

The Stranger's Voice

Meera stood frozen just past the threshold of the main hall. The wind outside pressed against the old wooden frame, making the windows creak like tired bones. The shadows around her seemed to close in, thickening with each passing breath. But it wasn't the house or the wind that unsettled her—it was the voice, calm, low, deliberate. And it had spoken her name.

She turned slowly, as if her limbs were wrapped in fog.

There, just beyond the half-open front door, stood a man. He didn't step forward. He didn't raise a hand or call again. He simply stood there, tall and unbending, like a statue shaped by secrets. The porch light behind him threw shadows across his face, but Meera could make out the sharp cut of his jaw, a faint scar above one eyebrow, and eyes that didn't blink and eyes that seemed to remember.

"I didn't mean to frighten you," he said, his voice quiet yet oddly sure. "But I needed to see you tonight. I've waited too long."

Her breath caught. "How do you know my name?"

"I've always known it," he replied, and though his voice held no threat, something in his words stirred an old unease within her. "Meera Sinha, daughter of Ashok and Nalini, born in the month of *Kartik* under the Rohini star. You belong to a line that was never meant to be broken."

She took a step back, her bare feet making the faintest sound against the cool tiled floor.

"Who are you?" she asked, her voice steadier than she felt.

The man didn't answer directly. Instead, he looked toward the courtyard, his face momentarily illuminated by the passing headlights of a car outside. "You've felt it, haven't you?" he asked. "The heaviness, the way the silence wraps tighter each night."

She didn't respond. Her heart was thudding. Her breath was shallow. It wasn't fear—not exactly. It was recognition, the way a forgotten dream tugs at your soul after waking.

"I need you to come with me," he said. "Not now, but at dawn tomorrow to the river, where the old stone steps descend into the water. Do you remember that place?"

Of course, she remembered. Her father had taken her there once when she was a child. Once reaching there, she said nothing and just watched the sunrise over the misty banks as temple bells echoed faintly across the water. She hadn't thought of that morning in years.

"Why?" she whispered.

"It is because if you don't, others will come. And they will not ask."

She glanced around. There was no phone, no signal, no one nearby. Only the rustling trees, the old walls, and this man who spoke in riddles.

"If you're lying..."

He raised a hand gently. "Then don't come. But if what I say rings even a sliver of truth in your heart, meet me. No one else can guide you through what's coming."

Before she could protest or ask more, he stepped back into the night. There was no sound of retreating footsteps, just the hush of the trees, the wind curling through the half-open door, and Meera—left standing between memory and mystery.

A Voice from the Past

Meera stepped back from the front door, her heartbeat echoing in her ears like temple bells struck out of rhythm. She hadn't imagined the voice. It was clear, deliberate, and eerily familiar. But who in this city—who in this life—could possibly know the name she had buried so carefully?

She approached the peephole. There was nothing. The walkway beyond the gate was still, disturbed only by falling neem leaves and the distant hum of a passing scooter. She hesitated, fingers resting on the door latch. Then, slowly, she cracked it open and peered out.

There was no one. But there—on the old stone steps—lay a white envelope.

She frowned. It hadn't been there earlier. There was no sound of footsteps, no ring of the bell, just the envelope, resting like a whisper from another time.

Cautiously, she picked it up. The paper was thick, textured, and almost ceremonial. There was a single name, handwritten on the front in a familiar blue ink:

Meera Sinha.

Her breath caught.

It wasn't the name that surprised her, but the fact that she hadn't heard it in years, and of course, the handwriting – That precise, flowing cursive, the long loop in the 'M', the gentle slant of the 'S', the subtle flourish on the final 'a'. She'd seen this style before in a notebook, on old postcards, on the inner flap of a tattered book of poems.

It was **Aarav's** handwriting.

The envelope trembled in her hands.

No. It couldn't be. Aarav was long gone. He was lost to a past life she had shed like an old skin. That chapter had closed in silence and pain. It had no business showing up now—certainly not in her new world, her carefully crafted stillness.

Yet the script was unmistakable.

She turned the envelope over. There was no stamp, no address, just her name.

Slowly, hesitantly, she opened it.

It was a handmade single sheet, with a handwritten verse:

"I saw you in the courtyard light,
Not a shadow changed, not time's spite.
The jasmine waits, the silence knows,
Some flowers wilt, but one still grows."

Her heart slammed into her ribs. She remembered this poem. Not because it was his—but because **she** had written it in a moment of heartbreak into the corner of her old college diary. She thought no one had ever read that poem.

But Aarav had read it years ago. She remembered now—he had found the page one late afternoon and told her softly, "You write like someone who sees souls."

He had memorized it.

Now here it was—reborn on paper, at her doorstep, like a ghost from her past walking barefoot into her present.

She sank onto the edge of the divan. The ceiling fan was humming softly, unaware of the storm that had begun to brew inside her.

If this were a message, it wasn't random.

Who knew the poem? Who knew the name? Who still had Aarav's handwriting?

More importantly, why now?

Outside, the silence returned, but inside Meera, something old and unfinished had awakened—and it was not going back to sleep.

No name, no explanation, but the poem—she had read it before. She had written it, long ago, in the margins of her college notebook. Aarav had once said it was the only verse that made him believe she could change the world.

Why now?

She looked around the silent room, half expecting him to be there, leaning against a doorframe with that old crooked smile. But there was only the hum of the fan, the stillness of her carefully curated life.

A chill crept up her spine.

This wasn't a coincidence. This was a message, a whisper from the past. A door creaked open when she had long assumed it had been bolted shut.

And she had no idea who—or what—stood on the other side.

Whispers from an Empty Room

The hallway outside Meera's room stretched ahead like a silent tunnel. The soft thump of her heartbeat seemed louder than her footsteps. She wasn't sure why she was walking toward the guest room—only that something had stirred inside her as if her name, whispered by the man at the gate, had pulled loose a memory long buried in the shadows.

She stood before the guest room door. It was slightly ajar. She pushed it open and stepped inside.

The room smelled faintly of old incense and sandalwood polish. The curtains billowed gently in the breeze, though the window was latched shut. Everything seemed exactly as she remembered from the morning: the neatly folded bedsheets, the water jug on the side table, and the untouched stack of old magazines.

Yet something felt different.

A low hum pulsed in the air—like an old radio left on between stations. She walked slowly to the desk and found her father's worn leather diary sitting open. That startled her. She was certain she'd locked it away months ago, after his passing.

Her breath caught.

On the open page was a name. It was her name, written in her father's firm, looping hand: *"Meera. Trust no one who speaks of orchids."*

She sat down, numb. The diary held no other entries after that. It was as if her father had scrawled the warning in a moment of urgency. The ink was smudged at the edge, as if written in haste—or fear.

A whisper curled through the room like smoke: "He told you, didn't he?"

She spun around.

No one was there.

Her chest tightened. Was she hearing things? Was the pressure of returning to this old house starting to unravel her senses?

She placed the diary back down and rose to her feet, shaking off the chill. She needed answers, not ghosts.

In the hallway, she spotted a shadow disappearing around the far corner. This time, she didn't hesitate. She followed it down the steps, through the inner courtyard, past the Tulsi altar where her mother used to pray.

It led her toward the old store room at the back.

Meera stopped. The door was ajar.

She hadn't opened it in years.

Inside, moonlight spilled across the dusty floor. And there, against the wall, was a shape wrapped in coarse brown cloth—a trunk she'd never noticed before.

She stepped in.

The air was thick and stifling.

As she crouched beside the trunk and ran her fingers over the rusted metal clasp, she felt the prickling sensation again—like someone watching her.

She turned.

Still there was no one.

And yet, she could almost feel a breath against her neck.

With a trembling hand, she opened the trunk.

Inside, beneath layers of newspaper and cloth, lay a set of old photographs of her father, a younger version of herself she didn't recognize and a man, the same man from the gate.

The Whisper beneath the Floorboards

Meera crouched low, the chill of the stone floor biting through her thin kurta. The room held its breath, the stillness so complete it almost rang in her ears. Her fingers traced the fine cracks between the wooden floorboards beneath the old rug, and she listened again.

That whisper. She hadn't imagined it.

A soft rustle—like a sigh from the past.

Her heart pounded. Tentatively, she knocked on the planks.

Once.

Twice.

The third knock met a hollow echo. Her breath hitched. It was subtle, but unmistakable.

She pulled the rug aside and ran her fingers along the edges of the worn wood. One board felt looser than the rest. Her fingers pried at the gap, splinters biting into her skin. With effort, the board creaked upward, revealing a narrow cavity beneath.

The musty smell of dust and forgotten years rushed out, mingling with the faint scent of sandalwood that still lingered in the house. Hidden inside was a bundle wrapped tightly in oilcloth, the fabric stained and brittle. Carefully, Meera drew it out and placed it on her lap, her hands trembling slightly, as if touching the past itself.

She unwrapped it with reverence, layer by layer, as if unveiling something sacred.

Inside were two things: a thick envelope, sealed with faded wax and tied with old twine, and a small blue velvet pouch, stained and worn. She opened the envelope first.

Inside were several letters, each written on yellowed parchment in an elegant, looping script.

The first one began: "My dearest Anandi,"

It was her mother's name. Meera's throat went dry.

She flipped to the end of the letter. "Yours forever, N. R."

N. R.?

She read the first few lines. The tone was intimate, filled with longing and tenderness. There was no mention of Rajan, her father. No clues about who N. R. was, except for a line that sent shivers through her spine: *"Keep the pendant hidden. If they find it, it will be the end of us both."*

Her breath caught as she opened the velvet pouch. Nestled within was a pendant—delicate, golden, shaped like a blooming lotus, with a tiny symbol engraved at its center. The symbol stirred something in her memory—faint, like a dream she couldn't quite hold.

Suddenly, the window flung open with a violent gust. Wind tore through the room, scattering the letters like startled birds. One page fluttered out into the hallway.

Meera scrambled after it, bending to pick it up just beyond the doorway.

That's when she heard it.

Sound of footsteps inside the house. It was slow, deliberate.

She froze. Every muscle in her body screamed for silence. She pressed herself against the wall, clutching the pendant and the letter.

In the reflection of the mirror at the hallway's end, she saw a figure move—a shadow, tall and still, just beyond the turn.

A chill wrapped around her like a second skin.

"Who's there?" she whispered.

There was no response.

Then came a voice—low, smooth, terrifyingly calm.

"You were never meant to find that."

Chapter 3

Shadows behind the Curtain

The Unseen Presence

The morning sun filtered softly through the delicate lace curtains, casting golden patterns that danced across the worn wooden floorboards of the ancient house. Meera sat by the window, the lotus pendant warm and heavy in her palm, her thoughts swirling like the drifting dust motes caught in the beams of light. The events of last night clung to her like a shadow she could not shake—the whispered warnings beneath the floorboards, the chilling voice that spoke her name, and the figure that moved just beyond the hallway's reach.

The house, once a sanctuary filled with memories of laughter and love, now felt like a maze of secrets waiting to be uncovered.

Her fingers closed tighter around the pendant, feeling the smooth coolness of the gold against her skin. The symbol delicately etched into its center was unfamiliar, yet it stirred something deep within—a memory just beyond reach, like a dream slipping away upon waking. It seemed to pulse faintly, as if alive with a heartbeat of its own, calling to her through the silence.

A soft creak from behind startled her, making her jump slightly. She turned quickly to see Kamala, the housekeeper, standing hesitantly in the doorway. The lines on Kamala's weathered face seemed deeper today, etched with worry and secrets she was reluctant to share. Her eyes flickered with caution, weighing the words she was about to speak.

"Appa's diary…" Kamala began, her voice barely more than a whisper, "You must be careful, Meera-ji. There are things in this house—things in the past—that are better left untouched."

Meera's gaze searched Kamala's, looking for truth in the hesitant silence that followed. "Why, Kamala? What don't I know? What are you afraid of?"

The older woman glanced toward the shadowed hallway, then back to Meera. "There are old stories, Meera-ji, stories about your father's past, about dangers and debts, promises made in darkness. There are those who would do anything to keep those stories buried forever."

A chill curled down Meera's spine, making her fingers tighten instinctively around the pendant. The weight in her hand suddenly felt heavier—laden with a history she had never been told.

Kamala's eyes dropped to the small golden lotus in Meera's palm. "Where did you find that?"

"In the storeroom," Meera answered quietly.

Kamala pressed her lips into a thin, grim line. "That pendant isn't just a trinket. It's a symbol, a symbol of loyalty, of promises kept—and broken, promises that sometimes come with a price far greater than we can imagine."

Meera swallowed hard, the gravity of Kamala's words settling around her like thick fog.

Outside, the breeze stirred the jasmine in the courtyard, their fragrance delicate yet haunting. Beneath the sweet scent, there seemed to be a darker note—an unseen presence lurking, watching.

Her eyes drifted back to the curtains, now gently shifting in the breeze, shadows creeping along the fabric like fingers reaching out. The sunlight dimmed as heavy storm clouds gathered on the horizon, promising rain and thunder.

There was far more hidden beneath these quiet walls than memories or dust, more than letters or whispered names.

And Meera was only beginning to uncover the first threads of a tangled story that would change everything.

The Unseen Visitor

The house had settled into an uneasy quiet as the afternoon stretched into dusk, shadows growing long and mysterious across the courtyard. Meera felt the weight of Kamala's words press down on her like an invisible cloak—warnings woven with fear and love, yet shrouded in secrecy. The golden lotus pendant rested heavily on the small wooden table beside her, its faint gleam the only light in the dim room.

She moved carefully through the rooms, each step echoing softly on the wooden floors, her senses alert to every creak and whisper. The scent of sandalwood mingled with the heavy perfume of jasmine from the garden outside, wrapping the house in a heady, almost intoxicating atmosphere. The old walls seemed to hold their breath, guarding secrets older than time.

Meera's thoughts churned with questions—Who was this mysterious N. R.? What promise did the pendant symbolize? And what dangers had her father hidden beneath a lifetime of silence?

Her fingers brushed the worn spine of her father's diary resting on a nearby shelf. She hesitated, heart pounding as she opened it once again. The neat handwriting spilled secrets onto the pages, fragments of a past she thought only she knew. Each word carried weight—truths and lies tangled together.

Suddenly, the stillness was broken by a soft knock at the front door. Meera's breath caught in her throat. No one had been expected, and the timing felt ominous. The knock came again—slow, deliberate, measured.

Cautiously, she approached the entrance, every instinct alert. Through the frosted glass, she saw a figure standing just beyond the threshold—a man cloaked in shadow, his features hidden by the fading light. Though she couldn't make out his face, there was something in his stance—quiet, deliberate—that unsettled her deeply.

"Who is it?" Meera called softly, trying to steady her voice despite the fluttering in her chest.

The man did not answer. Instead, he lifted a hand and held up a small, folded piece of paper. Without a word, he turned and disappeared into the fading light, leaving her with more questions than answers.

Meera's hands trembled as she picked up the note from the doorstep. The paper was old and worn, edges frayed from time. Unfolding it carefully, she read a single line scrawled hastily in dark ink: *"Trust no one. The past is never buried."*

A chill ran through her, colder than the evening air slipping through the cracks of the old house. The shadows lengthened, deepening as if the walls themselves were closing in.

She folded the note, tucking it into her pocket, her mind racing. Who was this visitor? What did he want? And what secret was he trying to protect—or warn her away from?

Meera felt the quiet house of her childhood transform beneath her feet. The shadows behind the curtain were no longer distant whispers—they were reaching out, pulling her deeper into a mystery that refused to let go.

Secrets in the Shadows

The evening wrapped the old house in a deepening cloak of twilight, softening the hard edges of the day and turning familiar corners into mysterious silhouettes. Meera sat quietly in the study, the folded note from the mysterious visitor pressed gently in her palm, her heart beating unevenly with a mixture of dread and determination.

Her eyes kept drifting to the golden lotus pendant resting on the desk beside her. It shimmered faintly in the dim light, as if containing a secret flame burning just beneath its polished surface. This pendant was far more than a mere keepsake; it was a symbol, a key to secrets her father had guarded fiercely and silently.

Her fingers traced the delicate carvings on the pendant's surface, feeling the cool metal warm beneath her touch. Memories surfaced—her mother's soft voice narrating tales of loyalty, courage, and sacrifice. These were tales Meera had admired but never fully understood until now. The weight of those stories pressed heavily on her soul, urging her forward despite the growing shadows swirling around her.

Outside, the restless wind stirred, rattling the old windowpanes with a soft, persistent murmur. Shadows flickered along the walls, dancing like restless ghosts in the fading light. Meera sensed a presence—unseen yet palpable—lurking just beyond the threshold, watching and waiting silently.

Summoning her courage, she rose and moved to her father's desk. The drawer groaned softly as she pulled it open, revealing a trove of old papers, yellowed photographs, and forgotten memories. She sifted through them, her fingers trembling slightly. Her eyes settled on a faded photograph of her parents standing side by side, smiles carefully composed but eyes heavy with unspoken truths.

Beneath the photograph lay a small, leather-bound journal. Meera opened it reverently, the fragile pages crackling softly. The writing was urgent, sometimes desperate—revealing a man wrestling with ghosts from his past, threats lurking in the shadows, and a promise made to protect something precious at all costs.

One entry, dated just weeks before Meera's birth, caught her breath sharply: *"The danger draws near. I fear for Anandi and the child. The pendant must remain hidden, or all will be lost."*

Her heart pounded as the weight of those words sank deeply in. The pendant was more than a symbol—it was a beacon, a promise, and a warning all at once.

Suddenly, a faint noise drifted from the hallway—a soft creak, barely audible but enough to send a shiver down Meera's spine. She froze, every sense alert. The house was no longer a sanctuary; it had become a stage for secrets long buried, and she was unwillingly at its center.

With trembling hands, she reached for the lamp and extinguished it, plunging the room into shadows deep and thick. Moonlight filtered through the window, casting silver patterns across the floor. Every shadow seemed alive, every whisper magnified in the heavy stillness.

Meera's resolve hardened. No matter the cost, she would uncover the truth hidden beneath the shadows—and face whatever darkness lay ahead.

The Whisper in the Dark

The night deepened outside, folding the house into a thick cocoon of shadows and silence. Meera stood by the window, watching the rain begin to fall in slow, steady drops, each one pattering softly against the glass like whispered secrets slipping into the dark. The soft murmur of the storm was both a comfort and a warning, wrapping the old house in a fragile veil of sound and shadow that seemed to pulse with its own quiet life.

Inside, the shadows grew heavier, pressing in with a silent intensity that made the very air feel thick and alive. The golden lotus pendant lay on the table, its faint glow barely visible beneath the flickering candlelight. Meera's fingers brushed its smooth surface, tracing the intricate carvings as she tried to steady her racing thoughts and calm the storm that churned inside her heart.

A sudden creak echoed sharply through the long hallway, breaking the silence like a knife slicing through velvet. Meera's breath caught, and she turned quickly toward the sound, her heart pounding like a furious drum in her chest. The house, with all its creaking bones and whispered memories, was alive in ways she could barely understand—an old sentinel guarding secrets that refused to stay buried beneath layers of time.

Slowly, she stepped into the corridor, the wooden floor cold and uneven beneath her bare feet. The scent of damp earth and old wood filled the air, mingling with the faint, lingering perfume of jasmine from the garden outside. Her eyes strained against the darkness, searching for the source of the noise, while the rain tapped steadily against the roof above, the rhythmic sound mingling with the quickened beat of her heart.

As she reached the end of the hall, a soft whisper drifted through the stale air—a voice so faint it might have been imagined, yet urgent and unmistakable. It spoke her name, barely audible but filled with an unyielding insistence that sent a chill down her spine: *"Meera..."*

She spun around, heart hammering fiercely, but no one was there. The house felt empty, yet charged with an unseen energy that seemed to pulse just beneath the surface. Shadows danced mockingly along the walls, flickering and twisting in the candlelight as if alive, weaving shapes that blurred the line between reality and nightmare.

Meera's mind raced with possibilities. Was it the trick of the storm, a figment of her anxious imagination, or something more? A ghost from the past reaching out, a warning from someone watching and waiting to step from the darkness? The questions echoed through her mind like footsteps in an empty hall.

Her fingers tightened around the pendant as if drawing strength and courage from its cold metal surface. The weight of the symbol steadied her breath and sharpened her resolve, grounding her in the swirling chaos of doubt and fear.

She knew one thing for certain—she was no longer alone in the house. The secrets that had long been buried were waking, stirring the shadows that clung to the walls like restless spirits. And with them came a presence that would not rest until the truth was dragged into the light, no matter the cost.

The Unseen Watcher

The storm outside had grown fiercer, rain lashing against the windows like a wild, relentless drumbeat. Inside the house, Meera felt the weight of silence settle around her, thick and heavy like a fog creeping through every corner. The golden lotus pendant rested cool and steady in her palm—an anchor in the swirling chaos of her thoughts and fears.

Moving cautiously through the dimly lit hallway, her senses were razor-sharp. Every creak of the old floorboards beneath her bare feet echoed loudly in the stillness. The soft whistle of the wind through the cracks in the windows was like a whispered warning. Meera's eyes darted anxiously to every shifting shadow, wondering if something unseen lurked just beyond her line of sight, waiting for the right moment to reveal itself.

The house seemed alive with secrets—echoes of half-forgotten stories and silent memories that clung to its very walls. Meera's pulse quickened as she approached the grand staircase, the heart of the old home. There, in the dim light, a flicker of movement caught her eye—a shadow slipping quickly at the edge of her vision, vanishing before she could fully focus on it.

Was she imagining things, or was someone truly watching her every step? The thought sent a chill down her spine.

She gripped the pendant tighter, drawing comfort and courage from its familiar weight. The feeling of being observed was both terrifying and strangely compelling. She knew she couldn't run from what was hidden in the darkness. She had to face it, whatever it was.

Her mind went to her father again—his last few days, the locked box in his room, the whispers that stopped when she entered a room. There were puzzles all around her, fragments of something vast and veiled. Could this watcher be part of that same pattern? An echo from her past? Or a stranger weaving himself into her story?

Her breath hitched as she stepped closer to the drawing room door. Something told her that beyond it, answers waited—answers she might not be ready for. But retreat was no longer an option. The sense of presence was stronger now, as if the walls themselves leaned in, listening to her footsteps, measuring her heartbeat.

Just then, a sharp, deliberate knock echoed through the house, reverberating from the front door. Meera froze, breath caught in her throat. Her mind raced—who could possibly come calling at such an hour, in the middle of a storm this fierce?

With trembling hands, she moved toward the door, each step heavy with anticipation and fear. The storm's fury howled louder, rattling the windows and shaking the ancient wood. As she reached out to grasp the doorknob, a sudden gust of wind blew through the house, snuffing out the candlelight and plunging the room into utter darkness.

In that moment of complete blackness, Meera felt the presence of the unseen watcher more keenly than ever before. Her heart thundered wildly in her chest, but she stood firm, refusing to retreat into fear.

Tonight, the shadows would no longer keep their secrets. Whatever or whoever had been watching, waiting—it was time for the truth to step into the light.

And Meera, for the first time in days, was ready.

Chapter 4

The Night She Vanished

The Last Sunset

The sun dipped behind the line of neem trees at the far edge of the courtyard, casting long amber shadows that stretched like sleepy limbs across the stone floor. Meera sat by the ancient swing, her bare feet brushing the dusty ground, a half-read book lying open on her lap. The breeze was gentle tonight, cool but not cold, carrying with it the scent of jasmine from the flower beds and something faintly smoky from a faraway kitchen fire. For a moment, the world was still — as if it too were holding its breath.

It was one of those evenings Meera would later remember — not for its beauty, but for its silence.

Inside the house, lamps were being lit. The flickering *diyas* in the hallway cast warm halos on the whitewashed walls. She could hear the soft murmur of Amma chanting the evening prayers from the puja room. Her voice was low, almost like a lullaby, weaving Sanskrit verses into the quiet dusk. Meera closed her eyes, letting the sound wash over her.

She didn't know then that it would be the last time she heard her mother's voice like that.

Ranga, the old servant, was sweeping the front porch. The soft scrape of the broom bristles on the red oxide floor was oddly comforting. He paused for a moment, looking at Meera with a mixture of affection and worry. He opened his mouth as if to say something, then thought better of it and resumed sweeping.

Meera stood up and stretched. The book slipped from her lap, forgotten. The pages fluttered in the wind like wings trying to take flight. She looked up at the sky. A single mynah bird flew overhead, calling out into the vast expanse, its voice sharp against the descending silence.

She felt something then — not fear, not yet — but a strange stillness, like the moment before thunder breaks. There seemed to be a pause in the rhythm of the day. It was the kind of quiet that doesn't feel natural.

Turning back toward the house, she saw a figure moving behind the curtain of her upstairs room.

Her brow furrowed.

Everyone else was downstairs. Her brother had gone to the market, Ranga wouldn't go upstairs without being asked, and Amma was in the puja room.

She stood there, eyes fixed on the thin white curtain as it fluttered in the breeze. The figure didn't appear again.

Perhaps it was a trick of the fading light, or perhaps not.

Meera stepped into the house slowly, her fingertips trailing along the cool wall.

Something had shifted, but she didn't know what. However, somewhere deep in her heart, a quiet voice whispered: *The night has begun.*

Above her, a pigeon cooed from its perch in the rafters. The clock in the hallway chimed softly—seven o'clock, the kind of hour when the world teeters between the real and the unreal. She glanced once more at the stairs leading up to her room. The curtain was still again.

But her heartbeat wasn't.

A Knock at Dusk

The knock came just as Meera reached the top of the stairs.

It was not loud, not hurried. There were just three measured taps — as if whoever stood outside knew they were expected.

She froze mid-step. Her eyes shifted from the corridor to the front door downstairs, and then back to the window at the end of the hall. The curtain in her room no longer moved. But the air around her felt heavier now, as if it had absorbed something unseen.

The knock came again—three soft raps that somehow echoed louder than they should have.

Amma, still in the puja room, didn't react. Ranga had disappeared, probably gone to the backyard shed. Meera stood uncertain, the beat of her heart now syncing with the rhythm of those knocks.

She turned slowly and descended the stairs. The lamps flickered as she passed, casting long shadows that danced on the walls. From the main door's frosted glass panel, she could see the silhouette of a man — tall, still, and waiting.

She opened the latch but kept the chain on. "Yes?"

The man leaned slightly toward the gap. "Is this the Srinivasan house?"

"Yes," Meera said slowly. "Who are you?"

"I have a message for you from your father."

Meera's spine stiffened. "My father's in Hyderabad."

The man nodded. "I met him there. He asked me to deliver something personally. May I come in?"

"No," she said, without hesitation. Something about his voice made her skin crawl — not harsh or threatening, but too calm, too rehearsed like a man reciting lines from a script.

"You don't need to be afraid," he added, sensing her unease. "You can call him if you like. Here." He reached into his coat pocket and pulled out a folded piece of paper. "Just take this."

Meera closed the door slightly, unclasped the chain, and then opened it just wide enough to take the note. As she reached out, their fingers brushed, and the first thing she noticed was that his hand was unnaturally cold — not from the weather, but from something deeper, something lifeless. It was the kind of cold that stays on your skin long after the touch is gone.

She shut the door quickly and locked it.

Back inside, she opened the note. It was written in her father's handwriting — that looping Tamil-English mix she'd seen all her life: *Meera, don't trust anyone. Stay close to your mother. I'll explain everything soon. Destroy this note after reading.*

Her breath caught. She looked again at the door — the man was gone.

There were no footsteps, no fading shadow.

Just silence.

She ran to the window and peered out, but the street was empty. Even the birds had gone quiet, as if holding their breath.

Then she noticed something strange. The note — it smelled faintly of camphor, the kind used in rituals and something else... something metallic like dried blood.

She went to the puja room, her steps shaky now.

"Amma," she whispered, her voice trembling. "Something's not right..."

Amma turned, holding a small brass lamp. "What is it, Meera?"

She opened her mouth to explain, to show the note.

But it was gone.

Her fingers were empty.

The Note under the Bed

The morning sun filtered through the gauze curtains, casting a fragile glow over Meera's quiet room. She sat on the floor, her back against the wall, knees pulled close, eyes fixed on the tiny, locked window she had come to dread. The illusion of morning brought no comfort anymore—it only reminded her how long she had been away from the life she knew.

A soft knock echoed from the other side of the door—three quick raps, as usual. Like every day, it was time for her breakfast. There was a plate of poha, a glass of warm water, and a peeled orange. But Meera didn't respond. The footsteps receded as always, leaving silence trailing behind.

She moved slowly to the tray, more out of routine than hunger. But today, something was different. The plate sat unevenly on the tray, slightly askew. When she lifted the plate, something fluttered beneath it—a folded square of yellowing paper.

Her heart thudded in her chest. She looked toward the locked door, then again at the note. With trembling fingers, she unfolded it.

"You are not alone. He's not who he says he is. Midnight. Look under the bed."

The words were scrawled in haste, slanted and messy. The ink had bled in places, as if written with urgency. Her breath caught in her throat. Who had left it? Was it a trap or a test?

Still, her eyes flicked toward the narrow space beneath the bed. She hadn't dared look under it in days—it was too dusty, too dark, too unknown.

She dropped to her knees and reached under slowly, her fingers brushing against rough wood, then cloth, and then something soft and folded. She pulled it out. It was probably a bundle of fabric wrapped around what felt like... paper?

She unwrapped the bundle, with her heart pounding. Inside were three items: a creased photograph, a thin metallic key, and a second note.

The photograph was old—maybe twenty years or more. It showed a woman who looked like Meera, with the same eyes and the same nose. She stood beside a man with a hard face and eyes full of secrets. They were outside an old *haveli*. On the back, in faded ink, were written the words: *"Gauri and Vikram — 1999."*

Meera blinked. Who were they? How were they connected to her?

The second note was shorter: *"The truth begins where memory ends. Use the key when you hear the bell."*

She sat back, stunned. The bell, the key, Gauri and Vikram — what did any of these mean? Was it a warning, or a clue?

And, most of all, **who** was helping her? And more chillingly, **who** was the "he" the first note warned her about?

Meera folded the photograph and both notes back into the cloth carefully. She hid it beneath her pillow, her heart racing with a mixture of fear and hope.

The walls hadn't spoken, but they were no longer silent.

Tonight, the shadows might finally move.

Footprints in the Rain

The evening sky darkened quickly, thick clouds rolling in like an ominous curtain drawn across the village. A distant rumble of thunder echoed faintly as the first drops of rain began to fall, pattering softly on the cracked tiles outside Meera's window. The air smelled of wet earth and promise — but also something more unsettling, as if the storm carried whispers from the past.

Meera stood at the window, staring out at the courtyard below. The dim light from the oil lamps flickered in the drizzle, casting long, wavering shadows. Her eyes searched the muddy ground where the footprints had appeared that morning, deep and clear — leading from the garden gate to the side door, then vanishing without a trace.

Who had made them? And why come at a time when the world was already full of secrets?

Her mind raced with questions, but the rain offered no answers — only the steady rhythm of falling drops, a metronome counting down to something unknown.

The wind picked up, stirring the leaves and sending a chill through the air. Meera wrapped her shawl tighter around her shoulders, the fabric damp against her skin. The scent of wet earth filled her nostrils, mingling with the faint aroma of incense burning somewhere nearby. Somewhere familiar, yet distant, like a memory just out of reach.

Suddenly, a soft, deliberate knock broke through the rain.

Her heart skipped a beat. She wasn't expecting anyone.

The knock came again. It was urgent yet cautious.

Meera's fingers trembled as she moved down the stairs to the back entrance. Her footsteps echoed softly against the worn wooden floorboards.

She reached the door and hesitated for a moment before gripping the handle. The door creaked open under her touch, revealing a soaked figure stepping inside — a young boy, no older than twelve, his eyes wide and shining with fear.

"Please," he gasped, "they're coming. You have to hide her."

Before she could ask who "they" were, he pressed something into her hand — a small carved wooden box, light but heavy with mystery.

The boy's voice faltered. "The bell... the bell will ring twice. Then... then you must be ready."

His voice trembled, and a shiver passed down Meera's spine. Questions swirled in her mind, but there was no time.

And just like that, he vanished into the night, swallowed by the rain and shadows.

Meera clutched the box tightly, rainwater dripping from her sleeves. Outside, the storm grew louder, the world drowning in shadows and secrets.

The night had only just begun.

The Silent Watcher

The house fell into heavy silence after the boy's sudden departure, as if the very walls were holding their breath in anticipation. Meera stood frozen near the door, the carved wooden box still clutched tightly in her trembling hands. The intricate patterns on its surface seemed to shimmer faintly in the flickering light of the oil lamp, each swirl and line whispering secrets she was not yet ready to hear.

Outside, the rain battered the roof with relentless fury, each drop sounding like a tiny drumbeat marking the passing seconds. Shadows stretched and contracted across the room, their shapes dancing and twisting as if alive. Every corner seemed to watch her, unseen eyes piercing the gloom.

The boy's words echoed in her mind, a haunting refrain: *"The bell will ring twice."* What did it mean? Was it a warning, a countdown, or a signal?

Her heart thudded wildly in her chest as she moved toward the small, barred window overlooking the courtyard. The night outside was a blur of rain and darkness, broken only by the faint glow of distant lamps. Then, through the downpour, she saw it—a figure standing motionless, half-hidden in the shadows.

It was the silent watcher.

The figure's presence sent a cold shiver down her spine. Was this person friend or foe? Protector or predator? Meera's breath hitched as the figure slowly raised a hand in a deliberate, beckoning gesture.

The first toll of the bell rang out—a deep, sonorous clang that vibrated through the house and echoed in her bones. Time seemed to slow, each second stretching taut like a drawn bowstring.

Meera's gaze darted between the window and the carved box in her hands. The object felt heavier now, charged with unseen power and promise.

Then, the bell rang again.

Two clear, resonant peals cut through the storm's roar.

A surge of adrenaline coursed through Meera's veins. She hugged the box to her chest, steeling herself for whatever was to come. The night was no longer just dark—it was alive, breathing danger and mystery in equal measure.

Suddenly, the sound of footsteps approached from the garden gate, muffled by the rain but unmistakable. Meera's pulse quickened as the silent watcher turned and vanished into the gloom, leaving behind a swirl of wet leaves and unanswered questions.

The shadows closed in tighter.

Meera whispered a silent prayer and took a deep breath, ready to face the storm that awaited her.

Part 2

The Whisper of Danger

Chapter 1

The Silent Warning

A Flicker in the Dark

The storm had passed, but the air still held a certain tension, thick with the weight of secrets. Meera stood in front of her mirror, her reflection distorted by the faintest tremor in the glass. She had always trusted her instincts, but something was off tonight. The world outside her window was quieter than usual, too still. Even the crickets, which usually filled the night with their ceaseless chatter, seemed to have fallen silent.

Her fingers lingered on the edge of the box the boy had given her, the strange wooden artifact that had somehow found its way into her life. There was something unsettling about it — something more than its weight and ornate carvings. She could feel it, as if the box itself carried a warning. She knew it wasn't just an object; it was a symbol, a clue, a piece of the puzzle she wasn't yet ready to solve.

She had always believed that objects, especially old ones, had a kind of energy to them. Her grandmother had once told her that the past lingered in every object, every place, like a whispering echo of forgotten moments. But this box was different. It felt alive, pulsing with an unseen force — a presence that hovered just beyond the edge of her understanding. Every time she touched it, she felt something stir inside her, something ancient and powerful.

She turned, her gaze falling on the old clock in the hallway. The ticking of its second hand seemed louder tonight, almost deafening in the otherwise quiet house. The bell that rang twice echoed once more in her mind. Meera couldn't shake the feeling that time was running out, that she was being drawn deeper into a web she didn't fully understand.

Her thoughts were interrupted by a soft rustling from downstairs. Meera's pulse quickened. She lived alone in the house now, but the sound was unmistakable — someone was moving about in the living room. She wasn't expecting anyone. Her parents were out of town, and the neighbors hadn't mentioned any plans to stop by. The unsettling thought that someone had entered the house without her knowledge made her heart race.

Suddenly, the silence was broken by a sharp knock at the door.

Her heart skipped a beat. Who could it be at this hour? The boy hadn't returned, and no one else knew about the box. The very idea of someone else knowing about it sent a cold shiver down her spine. The knock echoed again, more urgent this time, as if the person on the other side was growing impatient.

Meera cautiously approached the door, every step measured and deliberate. The floorboards creaked under her feet, the sound piercing through the silence of the house like a warning. She glanced once more at the mirror, watching as her reflection seemed to stare back at her with questioning eyes. Was it her imagination, or did the reflection look different?

Her hand trembled slightly as she reached for the door handle. The air felt thick, pressing in on her from all sides, and her breath caught in her throat. The door rattled slightly, as if something or someone was waiting on the other side. The knock had ceased, but the sense of presence, of being watched, was stronger than ever.

Meera knew that once she opened the door, everything would change. The mystery that had been quietly simmering in the background of her life was about to spill over, and she wasn't sure if she was ready for it. But one thing was certain: she couldn't turn back now.

The Visitor in the Shadows

The knock at the door echoed again, sharper this time, pulling Meera out of her thoughts. She hesitated, her hand still resting on the brass handle, cold against her palm. Whoever it was on the other side wasn't leaving. A flutter of unease swept over her as she wondered if her instincts had been wrong. The boy's warning, the strange feeling around the box, and now this — everything was starting to feel like a cruel game, and she was the unwilling pawn.

For a moment, she stood still, trying to steady her breath. Her mind raced. What was it about this moment that felt so familiar? She had been here before — not physically, but in a different way. It was the same sense of impending doom, the same weight pressing on her chest. Her eyes flicked to the mirror once more, her reflection barely visible in the dim light. The whisper of danger she had felt earlier was now growing louder, but she couldn't pinpoint the source.

She opened the door just a crack, enough to see who was on the other side.

A man, tall and lean, stood there in the rain-soaked dark. His features were hidden beneath the shadow of his hood, but his eyes — piercing, dark — locked onto hers with an unsettling intensity. There was something strangely familiar about him, like a fleeting memory that she couldn't quite grasp. Meera felt a chill settle over her.

"Good evening," the man's voice was smooth, almost too smooth. "I'm sorry to intrude, but I have something for you."

He reached into his coat pocket and pulled out a folded piece of paper, holding it out to her with an air of casual indifference. Meera didn't take it immediately. Her gut instinct told her not to trust him. But then again, her curiosity — that insatiable curiosity that had always driven her — urged her to know more.

"Who are you?" she asked, trying to keep her voice steady, though she felt her heart pounding in her chest.

The man didn't answer directly. Instead, he simply said, "A messenger. A friend, if you choose to accept me as one."

His words hung in the air, their meaning cryptic and ominous. Meera's eyes shifted from the paper in his hand to his face, searching for any hint of his intentions. But all she saw were those deep, unreadable eyes. They were the eyes of someone who knew too much — someone who had been watching her for far longer than she realized.

"Please," he pressed, his tone softening. "It's important."

She hesitated, and then reached out, taking the paper from his outstretched hand. The moment her fingers brushed against the paper, a shiver ran through her. She unfolded it slowly, her breath catching as she read the message scrawled inside: *"The bell has tolled twice. You have one hour."*

Her pulse quickened. The words didn't make sense, and yet they felt like a command, a threat. Meera's hand shook as she held the paper, her mind racing to understand what it meant. But before she could ask any more questions, the man turned and walked away, disappearing into the rain-soaked night as if he had never been there at all.

Meera closed the door, her heart hammering in her chest. What had just happened? And who was that man?

The Puzzle Begins to Take Shape

The rain continued its relentless drumming against the windows, but inside Meera's mind, the storm had already begun. She sat at the kitchen table, the crumpled piece of paper still clenched in her hand, the words burning in her thoughts: *"The bell has tolled twice. You have one hour."*

What did it mean? The cryptic message from the stranger had left her more confused than ever. The bell? What bell? She didn't know of any bell nearby that could have signaled anything of importance. Her mind raced back to the box — the one the boy had left with her. Was it connected? Was this a part of some larger plan she was unaware of?

She had heard the clock strike twice before, but it was only a clock in the hallway. It was nothing out of the ordinary, just a normal sound that signaled the passing of time. Yet, somehow, that sound now felt weighted, charged with meaning. The clock had struck twice many times, but tonight it felt like more than just the hour. She couldn't help but wonder if it was a countdown — an ominous reminder that something was about to unfold, whether she was ready for it or not.

She stood up, pacing the length of the room. The man's words echoed in her ears, as did the strange silence that had followed his departure. Her hand trembled as she touched her temple, trying to make sense of the disjointed thoughts that plagued her. Could she trust the stranger? What game was he playing?

Suddenly, there was a knock at the window.

Meera froze, her heart skipping a beat. No one had come to her window before, especially not in the middle of the night. She rushed to the curtain and peered outside, but the darkness was impenetrable, the rain blurring her view.

Her hands shook as she pulled the curtain back, but as her eyes adjusted to the dim light, her heart sank. There was no figure standing outside. No shadowy figure was watching from the other side. It was just the cold, relentless rain. Yet, something didn't sit right. The air felt heavier now, as if every movement was being scrutinized by some unseen force.

She shook her head and stepped back, her feet dragging across the wooden floor as she turned her attention back to the crumpled paper in her hand. She unfolded it again, tracing the words with her fingertips as if they might reveal more than they already had.

"The bell has tolled twice. You have one hour."

She read it again and again, as if hoping the words would rearrange themselves into something more clear. But nothing changed. She was no closer to understanding what this all meant. Was it a warning? A clue? Or had she been thrust into something much bigger than herself?

She looked back to the hallway, to the clock that still ticked its steady rhythm. The time now was 11:58 PM—only two minutes left before the clock struck zero hour. She felt the hairs on her neck stand up. Something was about to happen, and she had no idea what it would be.

The shadow flickered again, this time much closer, as though it was moving toward her. Her breath hitched. Her heart thundered in her chest. The doorbell rang, once, twice, the sound cutting through the heavy silence of the house.

The Doorbell's Toll

Meera's heart skipped a beat as the doorbell rang once more. There were two sharp chimes — deliberate, almost mocking in their precision. There was something undeniably menacing about them, something that suggested she was no longer in control of what was happening around her. The storm outside seemed to intensify, the wind howling like an animal trapped in a cage, adding to the eerie sense of impending danger.

For a brief moment, she stood frozen, staring at the door as if waiting for it to open on its own. The silence that had followed the knock was now replaced with an unbearable weight, as if every second stretched into eternity.

Her mind raced. Should she open the door? The stranger's visit was enough to unsettle her, but the ringing of the doorbell now felt like a direct challenge. She didn't know who was on the other side, but she couldn't ignore the gnawing feeling that her life was on the verge of a dramatic shift.

There was no turning back. She couldn't let fear control her.

With a shaky breath, Meera approached the door, each step slow and deliberate. Her hand trembled as she reached for the handle, her fingers brushing it lightly before gripping it tightly. She turned it, the mechanism clicking loudly in the stillness. As the door creaked open, the cold air from the outside rushed in, carrying with it the scent of damp earth and rain.

She peered out into the night, her eyes narrowing against the darkness. But there was no one in sight.

Just as she was about to close the door, she caught a glimpse of something in the corner of her eye. A shadow, fleeting yet unmistakable, was darting around the corner of the house.

A chill ran down her spine. Her instincts screamed at her to run, to shut the door and lock it. But she couldn't move. The shadow had seemed familiar, almost too familiar. Meera's thoughts raced as she tried to place it.

The figure was gone in an instant, swallowed by the night. But the feeling lingered—the sense that someone, or something, was watching her just out of sight.

Without thinking, Meera stepped outside. Her feet sank slightly into the soft ground, the coldness of the earth seeping through her shoes. She couldn't explain why she felt the need to follow the shadow, but some part of her knew that she needed to.

The house stood behind her, its windows like eyes watching her every move. She turned, scanning the darkened yard. There were no more signs of movement, but her heart pounded in her chest, urging her forward.

She took a few tentative steps and then stopped. There, in the far corner of the yard, she saw it — a faint glow, like the flicker of a dying candle. She squinted, straining her eyes to see through the thickening darkness. The glow was coming from behind the old shed, a place she hadn't ventured in years. It had always been abandoned, used only to store forgotten tools and items her father never cared to throw away.

Something was drawing her in. Against every rational thought in her mind, Meera found herself walking toward the shed, her footsteps steady but filled with hesitation. Each step felt like a decision she couldn't take back. The further she walked, the more the night seemed to close in around her. The air was thick with tension, as though the world itself was holding its breath.

As she neared the shed, the glow grew brighter. It was coming from a small crack in the shed's door, faint but unmistakable.

Meera hesitated for a moment. Then, with a steadying breath, she pushed the door open.

The Secrets behind the Shed

The door creaked open, and Meera stepped inside the shed, the musty smell of old wood and damp earth filling her nostrils. The flickering light was now much brighter, casting strange shadows on the walls of the small, cluttered space. Boxes and old furniture were scattered across the floor, some covered with dusty tarps, others abandoned and forgotten.

At the far end of the shed, she could make out a small table. On top of it was a single, flickering candle — the source of the strange light that had drawn her here. The soft flame danced erratically, as though disturbed by some unseen force, casting long, twisted shadows against the walls.

Meera's heart raced as she took a few cautious steps toward the table. There was something so eerie about the whole setup, something that made the hairs on the back of her neck stand on end. As she drew closer, her eyes fell on the object beside the candle: an old, tattered journal.

Her fingers trembled as she reached for it, lifting it gently from the table. The leather cover was cracked and worn, as though it had been handled by many hands over the years. The journal felt oddly heavy in her hands, as though it carried a weight far beyond its physical form.

She opened the first page.

"The truth is buried beneath lies." The words were written in a hurried, almost frantic hand. Meera's eyes widened as she read them, the weight of the sentence settling on her like a shroud. Was this some sort of clue? A warning? She turned the page.

"The bell tolls for those who dare seek the truth."

A chill ran down her spine. The message mirrored the one the stranger had left for her earlier: *"The bell has tolled twice. You have one hour."*

This was no coincidence.

Meera felt her pulse quicken. She flipped through the pages, her eyes scanning the words, each more cryptic and unsettling than the last. The journal spoke of secrets long buried, of a hidden truth that could change everything Meera thought she knew. It seemed to hint at something much larger — something that involved her, though she didn't yet understand how.

Suddenly, the candle flickered, casting a shadow on the walls that seemed to shift unnaturally. Meera froze, staring at the dark figure that moved behind her. She felt the temperature drop around her, as though the very air had thickened.

A soft noise behind her made her turn, her heart pounding in her chest.

Meera's breath caught in her throat as she slowly turned her head. Standing in the doorway of the shed was the figure she had seen earlier — the man with the dark, piercing eyes.

Her heart skipped a beat.

Chapter 2

The Man Who Knew Her Name

The Unseen Visitor

The morning after the strange events in the shed, Meera couldn't shake the feeling that something was terribly amiss. She went through her usual routine, but every corner of the house seemed to whisper of something she couldn't yet understand. Her thoughts were a tangled mess, each thread leading to more questions than answers.

As she prepared her breakfast, her phone buzzed on the kitchen counter. She picked it up without thinking, her mind still half-absorbed in the events of the previous night. It was a text message from an unknown number.

"You shouldn't have gone to the shed, Meera."

The message sent a jolt through her. How did they know? How could anyone know what she had done last night?

Her fingers froze on the screen, her heart racing. The message was chilling, as though someone had been watching her every move. But who? And why?

She quickly typed a reply, her fingers trembling slightly as she typed, *"Who is this?"*

The reply came almost instantly: *"I am the man who knows your name."*

Meera's breath caught in her throat. She stared at the message, her pulse quickening. The words were cryptic, yet chillingly familiar. He must be the man, the stranger. He had spoken with such certainty the night before, but this—this was beyond anything she had imagined. Was it a game? A warning? Or something far darker?

Her mind raced, but she couldn't form a coherent thought. Her fingers moved almost instinctively as she typed: *"Why are you doing this?"*

The reply was swift: *"Because you're not supposed to know. But now, there's no turning back."*

The words sent a cold shiver through her. The feeling of being watched — no, being hunted — crept over her like a suffocating fog. She dropped the phone onto the counter, the screen still glowing, but her mind was elsewhere. Her hands trembled as she reached for the glass of water on the counter, but the glass seemed heavier than usual, as if the weight of the world had suddenly shifted onto her shoulders.

She looked around the room, her eyes darting to the windows, the door, and even the shadows in the corners. She could feel a presence, though there was no one there. It was as if the walls themselves were closing in, the very air thickening with unease.

The clock on the wall ticked louder than usual, each second stretching longer than the one before. Her thoughts were a blur as she tried to make sense of it all. Who was this man? And why was he so determined to unsettle her?

The phone buzzed again, the message lighting up her screen: *"I'm closer than you think, Meera."*

A sharp knock on the door startled her, breaking her from the trance-like state she had fallen into. Her heart thudded painfully in her chest as she stood frozen, staring at the door. Who could it be? Was it him? The man who knew her name?

The Stranger's Voice

Meera couldn't shake the sensation that something terrible was about to happen. Her fingers hovered over the phone, yet she hesitated to pick it up. The screen still glowed, but the eerie silence that followed the last message weighed heavily in the room. It felt like the calm before a storm.

The knock on the door was still echoing in her mind, reverberating through the walls, but she couldn't move. She tried to steady her breath, forcing herself to gather the courage to confront whatever or whoever was on the other side.

A faint whisper of wind brushed against the window, sending a chill down her spine. Somehow, the house felt colder, the shadows seemed deeper, the corners were darker. Her pulse quickened, and the once comforting sounds of the world outside now felt alien and far away.

With a deep breath, she moved toward the door, each step heavier than the last. Her hand reached for the knob, her fingers trembling, but just as she was about to open it, another text arrived: *"I can hear your heart beating, Meera."*

Her stomach churned. It was him again, the man who knew her name.

She dropped the phone onto the counter, unable to bring herself to reply. The tension in the room felt suffocating now, as if something were pressing in from all sides. Her hand still hovered over the doorknob, but her body was frozen in place. Every instinct screamed at her to turn away, to ignore the knock, to pretend none of this was happening.

But her curiosity got the better of her.

Meera opened the door cautiously, stepping into the vestibule. The cold air rushed at her face, sharp and biting, as if the world itself were warning her. The street outside was empty, not a single soul in sight. The heavy shadows of the evening had already begun to descend, and the only sound was the soft rustling of the trees in the distance.

Yet, the feeling remained—the sense that something or someone was close.

She stepped further out into the yard, her eyes scanning the darkness. The lights of nearby houses flickered weakly in the distance, their warmth a stark contrast to the chilling sense of isolation she felt in her own home. She turned her gaze back to the front door, half expecting someone to be standing just behind her, waiting in the shadows.

But there was nothing.

As she slowly closed the door behind her, the hairs on the back of her neck stood on end. The silence was unbearable, but it was also familiar. The feeling—the sense of being watched, of being prey—was something she knew all too well. She had felt it before, but never quite like this, never so intense.

A strange noise broke her thoughts—a rustling sound, followed by the softest of footsteps. Meera turned, her heart racing.

Standing just a few feet away, in the dim light near the edge of the yard, was the same figure she had seen the night before.

His face was hidden in the shadows, but she could feel his gaze upon her, piercing and unwavering. The darkness seemed to swallow him whole, yet somehow, she knew he was there, watching.

Before she could react, the man spoke, his voice low and gravelly.

"I told you, Meera. There's no running from the truth."

Secrets in the Shadows

Meera's heart raced as she stood frozen in the yard, staring at the man in the shadows. His words still echoed in her ears, *"There's no running from the truth."* The chilling finality of his tone made it impossible for her to look away. Every instinct told her to retreat into the safety of her house, but her feet felt glued to the ground.

The man did not move. His figure was cloaked in darkness, yet there was a certain power that radiated from him. Meera could feel his presence all around her, in the very air she breathed, in the very space between them. The space felt so vast yet suffocating.

"Who are you?" Meera finally managed to whisper, her voice trembling despite herself.

The man remained silent for a moment, as though weighing her question. He slowly stepped forward, and for the first time, Meera could see a flicker of light catch his face. His features were sharp, angular, like those of a man who had spent a lifetime in the shadows. His eyes, dark and penetrating, were fixed on her with an intensity that made her breath catch in her throat.

"I am the one who will show you the truth, Meera," he said, his voice soft yet commanding. *"You may not believe it now, but you'll understand soon enough."*

Meera felt a chill run through her, though the night air was still and warm. She wanted to step back, to run, but something about him held her in place. His words, though cryptic, felt like they were tied to something deep within her—a hidden truth she had never known she was searching for.

"What truth?" Meera asked, her voice barely above a whisper.

The man took another step closer, his silhouette becoming more defined in the dim light. *"You've already begun to uncover it, Meera. But there's much more to discover. And you are not the only one searching."*

The words sent a wave of unease through her. She could feel the weight of his gaze on her, almost as if he were peering into her very soul. She wanted to ask more, to demand answers, but the words caught in her throat. It was as if she were afraid that speaking might make the truth more real—and she wasn't sure if she was ready to face it.

"Who are 'they'?" she finally asked, her voice faltering. *"And why do you know my name?"*

The man smiled, though the expression didn't reach his eyes. *"I'm not the one you need to worry about, Meera. Not yet. There are others who are far more dangerous. The ones you need to fear are already in your life. But they don't know you know."*

Her blood ran cold at his words. *"What do you mean?"*

The man's lips twisted into a thin smile. *"You'll find out soon enough."*

With that, he turned and walked away, disappearing into the darkness as swiftly and silently as he had appeared. Meera stood there, stunned, her mind racing with the weight of his words.

The truth. What was he talking about? And why did it feel like the world she knew was shifting beneath her feet, threatening to swallow her whole?

Meera stepped back into the house, locking the door behind her. The warmth of the room seemed like a distant memory as she leaned against the door, trying to catch her breath.

The quiet that followed was deafening. But it wasn't the peace of safety. It was the silence before the storm.

The Whisper in the Dark

Meera couldn't sleep. The night had stretched on endlessly, each minute heavier than the last. The unsettling conversation with the man had left her with more questions than answers, and as the hours passed, she felt the weight of those unanswered questions pressing in on her.

Her eyes flicked to the window, where the moonlight filtered in through the curtains, casting long shadows across the room. Everything seemed so still, so quiet. But beneath the surface of the silence, Meera could feel it—the presence that had lingered since that first message. It was as if the shadows themselves were watching her, waiting for her to make a move.

The sound of a creaking floorboard made her jump. Her heart raced, and she turned quickly, but there was nothing—only the dark, empty space behind her. She told herself it was nothing, just her mind playing tricks, but the fear gnawing at her wouldn't go away.

The house, once familiar and comforting, now felt like a maze of secrets, each room hiding something from her. She tried to shake off the unease, to focus on anything other than the creeping dread that seemed to follow her every move. But her thoughts kept returning to the man. Who was he? And what was he trying to tell her?

She picked up her phone again, checking for any new messages. There was nothing—no new text from the unknown number, no sign of the man who had appeared so mysteriously in her life. The silence was maddening.

Suddenly, the hairs on the back of her neck stood up. There was a soft whisper, like a distant murmur, that filled the room. It was faint at first, almost imperceptible, but it grew louder, clearer, until Meera could make out the words.

"The truth is closer than you think."

Her breath caught in her throat. The voice was so close, yet she couldn't see anyone. The whisper seemed to come from nowhere, wrapping around her like a dark cloud. It was the same voice—the same haunting presence from the shed, the same man who had sent her the strange messages.

"Who is this?" she whispered, her voice shaking with fear.

The whisper came again, this time louder and more distinct. *"I'm always here, Meera. Watching, waiting. The truth is buried beneath layers of lies, and you are the key to uncovering it."*

A chill ran down her spine. The words seemed to sink deep into her, like a dark seed taking root in her mind. She wanted to scream, to run, to do anything to escape the suffocating fear that gripped her, but she was paralyzed. The weight of the voice seemed to hold her in place, forcing her to listen, to understand.

For a moment, the whisper stopped, and Meera dared to breathe again. But just as quickly, the voice returned, more insistent now.

"You are closer than you think, Meera. All you have to do is open your eyes."

The whisper faded, leaving the room in oppressive silence once more. Meera stood frozen, her mind spinning. What was happening? Who was doing this to her? And why? The questions swirled in her mind like a storm, but there were no answers, only more whispers in the dark.

With shaking hands, she reached for the phone again, her fingers moving automatically as she typed a message to the unknown number: *"What do you want from me?"*

The reply came almost instantly: *"Everything."*

Meera's blood ran cold as she stared at the screen, her heart pounding in her chest. She had opened the door to something she couldn't close. The truth was out there, but it was a truth that might destroy everything she knew.

The Unseen Watcher

The phone buzzed again, jolting Meera from her thoughts. She looked at the screen, almost afraid of what she might find. It was another message. This time, it was more cryptic than the others: *"You've opened the door, Meera. Now you can't close it."*

The words hung in the air, heavy and ominous. Her heart pounded as she stared at the message, her mind racing. She had opened the door, but what had she let in? And how could she ever shut it again?

She glanced at the darkened windows, the quiet corners of the room, and once again felt that eerie sensation—the feeling that someone was watching her. But there was no one there. The shadows were silent, the house still. Yet, the sense of being observed never left her.

Meera stood and paced the room, her mind a whirlwind of fear and confusion. The man—the stranger who knew her name—had warned her that the truth was closer than she thought. But what truth? What was she supposed to uncover? And why her?

The questions kept tumbling in her mind, but they were like pieces of a puzzle that didn't quite fit together. She wanted to understand—to know what was happening—but the answers seemed to slip through her fingers like sand.

The phone buzzed again, this time more urgently. She grabbed it, her breath catching in her throat. It was from the same unknown number.

"You think you can escape, Meera, but you can't. You are already part of something bigger than yourself."

Her mind reeled. Part of something bigger? What did that even mean?

She stared at the message for a long moment, feeling the weight of it press down on her. The sense of dread, of being caught in a web she couldn't escape, filled her every thought.

Her finger hovered over the screen as she debated whether to reply. But before she could type anything, a new message popped up: *"You're not alone in this. But you will be soon."*

The final words struck her like a slap. She wasn't alone? Who else was involved? And why did that message feel like a threat?

The door to the house creaked behind her, and she spun around, heart racing. But once again, there was nothing—no sign of anyone—just the darkness and silence that seemed to follow her everywhere.

The realization hit her with the force of a thunderclap. The man wasn't just watching her; he was toying with her, pulling her into something she couldn't understand, something much bigger than her. And worse, she had no idea how to stop it.

Meera sank to her knees on the floor, the weight of it all pressing down on her. The room seemed to close in around her, and for the first time since this nightmare began, she felt completely and utterly trapped.

She reached for the phone one last time, typing a single question: *"Why me?"*

The reply was instantaneous: *"Because you are the only one who can see the truth."*

Chapter 3

Shadows behind the Curtain

The Unseen Presence

Meera's mind was still racing as she sat in the quiet of her living room. The events of the past few days—no, the past few hours—had been a blur, a whirlwind of messages, whispers, and shadows. She couldn't escape the feeling that something was happening, something beyond her control. And the worst part was that she didn't know who to trust.

The man who had appeared on her doorstep, the cryptic messages that seemed to come from nowhere, and now, the whispers in the dark — it was all too much. It was like a trap closing in around her, and the more she struggled, the tighter it became.

Her phone lay on the coffee table, still buzzing with notifications, but she couldn't bring herself to check them. The messages had become too much, too personal, too invasive. But she knew that no matter how much she tried to ignore them, they would still be there, waiting.

Meera glanced toward the window, half-expecting to see someone standing outside, watching her. The house felt different now—darker, somehow. The silence seemed deeper, and the shadows seemed to stretch farther. She shook her head, trying to clear the paranoia that was taking over.

As if on cue, the phone buzzed again, and Meera hesitated for only a moment before reaching for it. She had no choice. The pull to know, to understand what was happening, was too strong.

The message was short, almost too simple: *"It's not over yet."*

Meera's stomach dropped. She knew that meant something—something more than she wanted to admit. But what? What was the man trying to tell her? And why did it feel like she was on the verge of something terrible?

She stared at the message, the words burning into her mind.

It's not over yet.

But what wasn't over? What was she involved in? Her phone buzzed again. Another message, another cryptic line: *"They're closer than you think."*

The words struck her like a bolt of lightning: *They*. Who were *they*? The ones the man had warned her about? The ones who were closer than she thought? The sense of danger that had been lurking just beneath the surface suddenly felt all too real.

Meera's hands shook as she typed a response: *"Who are 'they'? What do you want from me?"*

She hit send, but as soon as the message left her phone, she regretted it. The last thing she wanted was to engage with this mystery man any more than she had to. But she had no choice. She had to know the truth.

The phone buzzed again. Her breath caught in her throat as she saw the reply: *"You're already part of it, Meera."*

The Unseen Visitor

The room felt unnervingly silent after the last message. Meera's fingers hovered over the phone, her mind racing with the words that had just appeared on her screen. *"You're already part of it, Meera."* What did that even mean? Had she been caught up in something far darker than she had ever imagined?

She tried to shake off the feeling, telling herself that it was just a sick game someone was playing. But deep down, she knew it wasn't. This was something real, something dangerous.

A soft knock at the door pulled her from her thoughts. It was so quiet, almost as if the sound had been muffled by the weight of the silence. Meera froze, staring at the door as if it might open on its own.

Who could it be? No one ever visited her at this hour. Not since... since everything started.

She glanced at the clock. It was well past midnight. Her heart pounded as she hesitated, torn between the need to stay hidden and the curiosity that urged her to open the door. Who was it? Was it him—the man who had haunted her dreams and sent her those chilling messages?

The knock came again, this time louder, more insistent.

Meera's breath caught in her throat. She didn't want to answer. Her instincts screamed at her to stay away, but she couldn't ignore the feeling—the pull that made her step toward the door.

She reached for the doorknob slowly, as if the action itself could summon something terrible. Taking a deep breath, she opened the door just a crack, enough to peer outside.

And there, standing in the dimly lit hallway, was a figure she didn't recognize.

The man was tall, his face partially obscured by a hood. His eyes were the only part of him visible, dark and intense, fixed on her with an almost unnatural focus. There was something unsettling about the way he stood there, like a shadow carved out of the night.

Meera felt a chill run down her spine, but she couldn't look away.

"Can I help you?" she asked, her voice trembling despite her efforts to remain calm.

The man didn't answer immediately. He just stood there, his gaze never wavering from hers. Meera's heart raced in her chest as the seconds stretched into what felt like an eternity.

Finally, he spoke, his voice low and gravelly. *"You've been asking questions, Meera. It's time to get some answers."*

Meera's breath hitched. The words sounded too familiar, too similar to what the other man had said—the one who had sent her the cryptic messages. She tried to open her mouth to respond, but the words wouldn't come. Her throat had gone dry, and she could barely breathe.

"Who are you?" she finally managed to whisper.

The man tilted his head slightly, as if considering the question. *"Does it matter?"* he replied cryptically. *"The truth is what matters now. And you've already started to uncover it."*

Meera swallowed hard, her mind racing. She wanted to slam the door shut, to escape this nightmare, but something kept her frozen in place. The man was right. She had started uncovering something, something that was drawing her in deeper than she had ever intended.

"What do you want from me?" she asked, her voice cracking.

The man's expression softened just for a moment, and then he stepped back, his face still hidden in the shadows. *"We'll talk soon enough. But for now, be careful, Meera. There's more at play here than you realize."*

Before she could say anything else, he turned and disappeared into the dark corridor, leaving her standing in the doorway, her heart racing in her chest.

Meera closed the door with trembling hands, locking it behind her. But even as she stood there, listening to the silence of the house, she couldn't shake the feeling that the night was far from over. The shadows were closing in, and there was nowhere left to hide.

Secrets in the Shadows

Meera sat in the quiet of her living room, her thoughts racing in a thousand directions. The encounter with the man at her door had shaken her more than she cared to admit. His cryptic words echoed in her mind, and she couldn't shake the feeling that she was caught in the middle of something much larger than herself.

"You've already started to uncover it." What was he referring to? What was she uncovering, and how was she supposed to stop it once she found out the truth?

The house, once her safe space, now felt suffocating. The walls seemed to close in around her, the shadows stretching longer with each passing minute. She stood up, pacing the room, trying to clear her thoughts. But nothing made sense.

She glanced at the phone again. It was another message. It was from the same unknown number, the one that had been sending her those unsettling texts.

"They're watching you, Meera. They always have been."

She froze. Her hand shook as she held the phone, the message flickering on the screen: *They*. Who were *they*? And why did it feel like her every move was being monitored?

A chill ran down her spine as she looked around the room, half-expecting to see someone standing in the shadows, watching her. But there was nothing—just the same empty silence that had been creeping up on her for days.

Meera's mind kept circling back to the same questions: What was going on? Why was she involved in this? The deeper she dug, the more tangled the web seemed to become.

Her fingers hovered over the screen, but she couldn't bring herself to reply. What could she say? What did she even want to know?

A noise outside the window caught her attention. It was faint at first, like a soft tapping. She moved cautiously toward the window, her heart beating faster with each step. As she drew closer, the tapping became louder, more insistent.

She peered through the blinds, her breath caught in her throat. There, in the darkness outside, she saw a figure standing in the yard—a shadow in the night, barely visible against the blackness beyond the window.

Meera's heart skipped a beat. She couldn't see the figure clearly, but she knew—it was the man, the same one who had been haunting her thoughts. But how had he gotten so close without her hearing him?

She stepped back from the window, panic rising in her chest. What did he want now? And why was he watching her so closely?

The phone buzzed again, the screen lighting up with a new message: *"The truth is closer than you think, Meera. But you're not ready for it yet."*

The words sent a wave of dread through her. It was as if the man was toying with her, pulling her in deeper into a mystery she couldn't understand, and might never be able to escape.

Meera turned away from the window, her mind racing. She couldn't sit here, waiting for something to happen. She needed to know what was going on—she needed to find answers.

Without another thought, she grabbed her coat and headed for the door. She didn't know where she was going, but she had to get out. The silence of the house was closing in on her, and the fear of being watched was too much to ignore.

The door closed behind her with a soft click, and as Meera stepped into the cool night air, she couldn't shake the feeling that she was being led somewhere. The question was: Where?

The Whisper in the Dark

Meera's footsteps echoed in the empty streets as she walked, the cool night air biting at her skin. The farther she walked from her house, the more the oppressive feeling of being watched seemed to fade. She hadn't realized just how suffocating it had become inside those walls.

But as she turned the corner, a shiver ran down her spine. The street was empty, but she couldn't shake the sensation that something was lurking just out of sight. The hairs on the back of her neck stood up, and every instinct screamed at her to turn around, to go back home where it was safe.

But the thought of that man, the mysterious stranger who seemed to know everything about her, kept her moving forward. She had to know more. She couldn't just run from this. Not when she was so close to uncovering the truth.

She stopped at the corner, her breath coming out in visible puffs in the cold air. A part of her wished she could go back to the comfort of her home, to bury herself under the covers and pretend this was all just a nightmare. But she knew that was impossible. The truth has a way of finding you, no matter how much you try to hide from it.

A flicker of movement caught her eye. Meera turned sharply, but when she looked, there was nothing there—no one—just the empty street stretching out before her, bathed in the soft glow of streetlights.

"Get a grip, Meera," she muttered to herself, trying to steady her breathing.

She was just being paranoid. It was all in her head. Right?

But then, the whisper came. It was soft at first, barely more than a breath in the night air, but it was enough to make her stop in her tracks. She strained to listen, but the street was silent again, as though nothing had happened.

The whisper came again, this time clearer. *"You can't run from the truth."*

Meera's heart skipped a beat. Her eyes darted around the empty street, searching for any sign of movement, but there was nothing. There was no one in sight. Yet, she knew she wasn't alone.

A cold chill settled over her as she realized that the voice wasn't just a sound in the wind. It was something or someone speaking directly to her. Was it the same man who had been sending her the cryptic messages? Was it the same presence that had been haunting her thoughts?

The fear that had been gnawing at her now felt like a solid weight in her chest. She had to get away. But she couldn't shake the feeling that wherever she went, the shadows would follow. The man would follow.

She took a deep breath and began walking faster, her footsteps quickening as she tried to outrun the growing dread. But the whisper came again, this time louder, more insistent: *"You can't escape. You belong to this."*

Meera's pulse raced as she broke into a run, her breath coming in ragged gasps. She wasn't sure where she was going, but she had to get away from the voice, from the shadows that seemed to be closing in around her.

Her feet pounded the pavement as she turned another corner, her mind racing with thoughts she couldn't control. What did it all mean? Who was behind this, and why her?

But no matter how fast she ran, no matter how hard she tried to outrun the fear, it was always there, just behind her, like a dark cloud on the horizon. And the whispers, they never stopped.

"You can't run from the truth."

The Unseen Watcher

The city felt different in the dead of night. The usual hum of life seemed to vanish, leaving only an eerie silence that weighed heavily on Meera's chest. Her breath came in shallow gasps as she continued running, the fear she had been trying to outrun only growing stronger with every step.

She could hear nothing but the sound of her own heartbeat in her ears, pounding like a drum. Her mind was a blur, racing through a thousand scenarios, none of which was good. Who was this man? How did he know so much about her? And why couldn't she escape from him?

The more she ran, the more the fear began to cloud her thoughts. She had to stop. She couldn't keep running forever. But the thought of going back, of returning to the place where the whispers had started, made her stomach churn with dread.

Her legs burned with exhaustion, but she didn't dare slow down. She had to keep moving, keep running.

As she turned another corner, her eyes caught a glimmer of light in the distance. It was a streetlight. It was faint, but it gave her something to focus on, something to head toward. She quickened her pace, desperate to reach the safety of the light.

But as she got closer, she noticed something strange. The streetlight seemed to flicker, casting long, twisting shadows on the pavement. Meera's heart skipped a beat as she slowed down, her senses heightened. There was something wrong about the way the shadows moved, like they were alive, stretching out toward her with a will of their own.

She stepped back, her breath catching in her throat. That's when she saw him again—the man. He was standing just beyond the streetlight, his face half-shadowed, his eyes locked on her.

He was the same man who had been sending her the messages, the same man who had been watching her.

"Who are you?" Meera's voice was barely more than a whisper, but it felt like a shout in the silence.

The man didn't move. He didn't speak. He just stood there, as if waiting for something.

Meera's pulse raced as she stepped back, her mind screaming at her to run. But her legs wouldn't move. She couldn't tear her gaze away from him.

Then, he finally spoke, his voice low and filled with an unsettling calm: "The truth is right in front of you, Meera. All you have to do is open your eyes."

His words were like a weight on her chest, crushing the air out of her lungs. She wanted to shout, to demand answers, but all she could do was stand there, frozen in place.

The man took a step toward her, his movements slow and deliberate. Meera's heart skipped a beat as she took a step back, her back pressed against the cold stone of the building behind her. She had nowhere left to run.

"You're already part of this," he said, his voice carrying an almost prophetic tone.

Meera shook her head, panic rising within her. "I don't understand. What do you want from me? Why are you doing this?"

He didn't answer immediately. Instead, he reached into his coat pocket and pulled out a small, folded piece of paper. He held it out to her, his fingers barely moving as if he was waiting for her to take it.

With trembling hands, Meera took the paper, unfolding it carefully. The words written on it were simple, but the meaning behind them was anything but: *"You have no choice now. The game has already begun."*

She looked up, but the man was gone. In his place, there was only the empty street, bathed in the dim light of the streetlamp.

Meera stood there for a long moment. The weight of the paper in her hand felt like a heavy anchor pulling her down. She couldn't understand it. She didn't know what was happening. But she knew one thing for sure.

Her life was no longer her own. The game had begun.

Chapter 4

The Darkness Unveiled

The Encounter in the Alley

The streets had become strangely quiet, the usual clamor of the city now muffled by an unsettling calm. Meera had walked for what felt like hours, each step drawing her farther away from the shadows that had followed her for so long. But the sense of unease still lingered, like an invisible hand at her back, pushing her forward.

She turned into an alley, one that seemed familiar in a way she couldn't place. It was narrow, with high walls on either side, and the only light came from a flickering streetlamp at the far end. The air was thick, heavy with the scent of dampness and decay. Meera pulled her coat tighter around her shoulders, instinctively quickening her pace.

Something wasn't right. She could feel it in her bones. Every nerve in her body screamed at her to turn around and leave, but her feet kept moving, as though they had a mind of their own. The alley was narrow, and the walls seemed to close in around her, making the night feel even darker than it already was.

She paused for a moment, taking a deep breath, trying to calm the rising panic in her chest. *Get a grip, Meera,* she told herself. *You're just tired. You've been through a lot. This is nothing.*

But just as she turned to leave, she heard the sound—a soft scuff of shoes against the pavement. It was faint at first, almost imperceptible, but it was there. She stopped dead in her tracks, her heart leaping into her throat.

Who's there?

There was no answer, only the sound of footsteps growing louder, closer. Meera's mind raced as she glanced around, but the alley was still empty. The light from the streetlamp flickered again, casting long shadows across the ground. Her pulse quickened, and a chill ran through her as she realized the footsteps weren't coming from behind her—they were coming from ahead.

The sound grew louder and faster, as though someone or something was approaching at a speed just beyond her reach. Meera's breath quickened, her eyes darting from shadow to shadow, searching for any sign of movement.

Just keep calm. Don't panic. It's just a person.

But the rational part of her mind, the part that had been keeping her calm all along, was slipping away. She wasn't sure if she was imagining it, but it felt as if the shadows in the alley were shifting, moving closer to her with every step she took.

Turn around, Meera. Get out of here.

She could feel her legs trembling now, the fear tightening around her chest like a vice. She wasn't sure how long she had been standing there, frozen, but she knew she couldn't stay much longer. She had to move. She had to get out.

With one last glance toward the alley's entrance, she made her decision and turned back toward the street. But just as she did, a figure emerged from the shadows.

It was a tall man, with a dark silhouette that blended with the night. He stepped forward with such suddenness that Meera had no time to react. Her breath caught in her throat as the man moved closer, his eyes glinting in the dim light of the streetlamp.

"Meera," he said her name with a cold certainty, as though he had been waiting for her.

Her heart skipped a beat, and she took an instinctive step back. "Who are you?" she demanded, her voice shaking more than she had intended.

The man didn't answer immediately. Instead, he seemed to study her, his gaze penetrating in a way that made her feel as if he could see through her, into the very depths of her soul.

"I've been looking for you," he finally said, his voice low, almost a whisper. "You've been running from the truth, but you won't be able to outrun it much longer."

Meera's mind raced. This wasn't the first time someone had said something like that to her. But the way this man spoke, the coldness in his voice, made her blood run cold.

"Who are you?" she asked again, more forcefully this time, her heart pounding in her chest. "What do you want from me?"

He stepped closer, and Meera instinctively took another step back, her feet pressed against the cold, wet stone of the alley.

"You've already started," he said, his voice a whisper of a threat. "The game has begun, Meera. And there's no way out."

A Glimpse into the Abyss

Meera's heart pounded in her chest as she tried to steady her breath, her legs still trembling from the encounter. She had barely registered the man's words before he disappeared back into the shadows, leaving her with nothing but the cold, empty alley and the weight of his cryptic message hanging in the air.

The game has begun—the words echoed in her mind like a drumbeat, and no matter how hard she tried, she couldn't shake them off. What did he mean by that? What was this game he kept talking about? And why her?

The questions swirled in her mind like a storm, each one feeding the anxiety that had settled deep in her chest. She had been running from something—she wasn't sure what—but every step she took seemed to pull her deeper into this strange, dangerous world.

She couldn't ignore it anymore. Whatever this man was trying to show her, whatever game had already begun, Meera knew she couldn't run forever. She had to face it. But how? Where did she even start?

The alley felt colder now, the darkness pressing in around her like a living thing. She needed to get out. She needed to get back to the safety of her apartment, to try to piece together everything that had happened over the past few days. But as she turned to leave, something stopped her. She felt a whisper just out of reach.

Meera froze, her pulse spiking once again. There, at the far end of the alley, a shadow moved. It wasn't the flickering, shifting kind she had grown accustomed to. This was a real figure, standing tall and unmoving. Her breath caught in her throat as she squinted into the darkness, trying to make out any distinguishing features.

It wasn't until the figure took a step forward that she realized who it was.

It was a man. But it wasn't the same man who had just spoken to her. This man was different—his face hidden beneath a hood, his body cloaked in shadow. He moved with a predatory grace, his steps calculated, each one bringing him closer.

Meera instinctively stepped back, but before she could react, the figure spoke, his voice smooth and low. "You're not alone, Meera," he said, his tone filled with quiet menace. "You've never been alone."

The words sent a chill down her spine. What did he mean? Was there someone else behind all of this?

The man didn't give her time to respond. He took another step closer, his presence overwhelming. She wanted to run, but her feet wouldn't move. It was as if the very air around her had thickened and grown heavier, making it impossible to breathe.

"I've been watching you," the man continued, his voice almost soothing in its calmness. "You're part of something much bigger than you think."

Meera opened her mouth to speak, but no words came out. She was paralyzed, caught between the need to understand and the overwhelming fear that had her rooted to the spot.

The man reached into his coat pocket and pulled out a small, rectangular object. He held it out to her, the cool metal gleaming in the dim light. Meera didn't move to take it, but her eyes were fixed on the object, trying to make sense of it. It was a small black box, the kind that looked ordinary at first glance but felt far from it.

"You don't have much time," the man said, his voice dropping lower. "Take it. You'll need it."

Meera hesitated, her mind racing. She could feel the weight of his gaze, the intensity in his words, but she didn't know if she could trust him. What was he really offering her? What was inside the box?

With trembling hands, she reached out and took the box, its cool surface sending a strange shiver through her. As soon as her fingers closed around it, the man turned and began to walk away, disappearing into the darkness without a word.

Meera stood there for a moment, frozen in place, the box clutched tightly in her hand. She couldn't understand what had just happened, but she knew one thing for sure.

Her life was no longer her own.

The Shattered Mirror

The box felt impossibly heavy in her hands as Meera walked away from the alley. It wasn't just the weight of the object, though—there was something far deeper pressing down on her chest. She couldn't shake the feeling that everything had changed in those few moments. What had just happened? And why did she feel as if the very fabric of her reality had been altered?

The city had never felt more foreign to her. The streets, once so familiar, now seemed like a maze of endless possibilities and dangers, each corner hiding an unknown truth. She had always thought of herself as someone who could handle anything, but now she felt as though she were walking in the dark, blindfolded, with no idea where she was going or what awaited her.

She needed answers. She needed to understand what was happening to her.

With shaky hands, Meera pulled the small box from her coat pocket and stared at it. The metal gleamed in the faint light, cold and unyielding. Her mind raced with questions, but the fear that had gripped her heart since the encounter in the alley kept her from opening it. What if it was something dangerous? What if it held the key to a nightmare she wasn't ready to face?

She couldn't just ignore it. Whatever this man had wanted her to see, to know, it was now in her hands.

Her fingers trembled as she lifted the lid, bracing herself for what was inside.

To her surprise, there was nothing but a single sheet of paper, folded neatly in half. It wasn't a letter—at least, not in the traditional sense. The paper was plain, almost too ordinary, but the words written on it were anything but: *The truth will set you free, but it will cost you everything you know.*

The words were scrawled hastily, as though they had been written in a hurry. Meera's breath caught in her throat as she read them again. The truth. It was always about the truth, wasn't it? But what truth? And why did it sound so ominous?

A sudden chill ran through her, as if the room around her had become impossibly cold. She glanced up, as if expecting the man to be standing right in front of her. But there was no one. The city was still, and she was alone.

The silence was deafening.

The truth will set you free...

But what did that mean for her? What truth was she supposed to uncover? What did she need to give up in order to be free of whatever trap she had found herself in?

Meera closed her eyes for a moment, trying to steady her racing thoughts. It felt like the walls around her were closing in, suffocating her. She couldn't breathe, couldn't think straight. She was caught in the middle of something far too big for her to comprehend. But she couldn't run anymore.

She had already crossed the point of no return.

The sound of her phone vibrating in her pocket pulled her out of her thoughts. She jumped at the sudden noise, her heart racing again. She reached for it quickly, her fingers brushing the edge of the screen. She didn't recognize the number. She almost didn't answer, but something told her she needed to.

With a deep breath, Meera pressed the screen, bringing the phone to her ear.

"Hello?"

There was a pause.

"Meera," came the voice. It was familiar, but she couldn't place it. "We know what you're trying to do."

The hairs on the back of her neck stood up. Who was this? How did they know her name?

"You're already too deep into this," the voice continued, low and urgent. "There's no way out now. But we can help you. All you have to do is trust us."

Before Meera could respond, the line went dead.

She stood there, staring at the phone, the weight of the conversation hanging in the air like a thick fog. The sense of unease from earlier came crashing back in full force. She had been given a choice, a path to follow, but it was a path lined with shadows.

There was no going back.

The Echo of the Past

Meera's heart raced as she stepped into her apartment, the door clicking shut behind her with a hollow sound. The events of the past few hours felt like a blur, but they weighed heavily on her mind, each detail pushing her deeper into confusion and fear. What was she involved in?

And why did it feel as though she was being pulled into a story that was already written, a story where she had no choice but to play a part?

She moved slowly through the apartment, her fingers trailing along the walls as if she were searching for something, anything, to ground her. The silence inside her home felt suffocating, as though the very air had thickened in her absence. The box—the one that had started this entire chain of events—remained clutched in her hand, its weight never easing.

She finally reached the living room and set the box on the coffee table, staring at it as though it might hold the answers to the questions she had been asking all night. The small black box sat there, innocent and unassuming, yet it seemed to pulsate with an energy she couldn't explain. The message inside, *"The truth will set you free, but it will cost you everything you know,"* kept echoing in her mind, refusing to let her rest.

The truth? What truth? Was this some kind of test? Some twisted game meant to break her, to push her to the edge of her sanity?

Meera sank into the couch, running her fingers through her hair. She needed answers, but they were just out of reach. She didn't know where to start—didn't know who to trust. The man in the alley, the voice on the phone, even the cryptic message inside the box—it all felt like too much, too fast.

She glanced around the room, the silence almost unbearable now. Everything felt wrong, as though her apartment wasn't even hers anymore. There were memories here—moments of peace and contentment—but they seemed distant now, like echoes of a life that no longer existed.

Meera's eyes landed on the bookshelf across the room. It was filled with old journals, books she had collected over the years, and photographs of her family—her father, her mother, and her younger brother. She hadn't looked at them in months, but now they seemed to call to her, a quiet reminder of who she was before all of this began.

Her gaze softened as she approached the shelf. She pulled down a small photo album, the leather cover worn from years of use. She opened it to the first page, her fingers lingering over the photos. Her mother's smiling face, her father's serious expression as he stood in front of their old house—each picture was a piece of a past she hadn't thought about in so long.

But as she flipped through the pages, something caught her eye—a photograph she didn't remember seeing before. It was a picture of her parents, standing with a man she didn't recognize. They were at some kind of event—a celebration, maybe—but there was something unsettling about the image. The man's eyes were dark, cold, and his smile was too wide, too knowing. There was an air of familiarity in the way he stood next to her parents, but it was off—like he belonged there, but also didn't.

She felt a chill crawl up her spine as she stared at the photograph. Who was this man? And why had she never seen this photo before?

Her hands began to tremble as she turned the page, desperate for an explanation. But the answers weren't there—only more questions.

The ringing of her phone broke her out of her thoughts. She jumped, startled, and quickly grabbed the device from the coffee table. Her heart skipped a beat when she saw the name on the screen.

It was the same number from before.

She hesitated for only a moment before answering.

"Hello?" Meera's voice was steady, but her insides were churning with anxiety.

"We need to talk," the voice on the other end said, the tone serious. "Meet us at the old church on Willow Street. It's time for you to know the truth."

The line went dead before Meera could respond, and she was left holding the phone to her ear, the words of the mysterious caller ringing in her head.

The truth—those same words that had been haunting her all night.

With a sinking feeling, Meera realized that whatever had begun, whatever game she was now a part of, it was only going to get darker from here.

The Unraveling Thread

The phone call had left Meera reeling, her thoughts tangled in a web of confusion and fear. The voice on the other end had been too calm, too confident—like they knew something she didn't. Something she needed to know. And they had demanded her presence at the old church on Willow Street. She didn't even know why she was listening, but deep down, she knew she had no choice.

The church was abandoned now, its once-grand stone structure falling into ruin. It had been years since anyone had attended services there, but that didn't make it any less imposing. Meera's footsteps echoed eerily as she made her way down the overgrown path leading to the entrance, the darkening sky casting long shadows on the ground.

She had been here before, many times as a child, her parents taking her to Sunday services and community events. It had always felt safe, comforting even, but tonight, the place felt different. It felt cold, as though the air itself was holding its breath, waiting for something to happen. Meera paused just before the doors, the weight of the situation pressing down on her.

What was she doing here?

She had been on edge all day, but now, standing before the church, it felt like something was about to break wide open. The air around her was thick with tension, and her heart pounded in her chest as if urging her to turn and run. But she couldn't. Not now. She had come this far, and there was no turning back.

Taking a deep breath, Meera pushed open the large wooden doors of the church. The sound of the hinges creaking in the silence made her skin crawl. Inside, the church was dimly lit by the faint glow of candles scattered across the pews. The air smelled of dust and old wood, and the faintest trace of incense lingered in the air, almost like a memory of something sacred.

In front of the church, there stood a figure. He was tall, cloaked in shadow, and for a moment, Meera wondered if she had made a mistake coming here. But then the figure turned, and she saw his face—his dark, cold eyes staring back at her.

"You came," the man said, his voice calm, measured. "I knew you would."

Meera swallowed, trying to steady her nerves. "Who are you? What do you want from me?"

The man smiled, but it wasn't a comforting smile. It was the smile of someone who knew far more than they should. "What do I want? I want you to see the truth, Meera. I want you to understand why you're here and what's at stake."

He took a step forward, his dark figure advancing slowly through the candlelight. Meera took a step back, but her feet were rooted to the floor, her body refusing to move.

"What truth?" she demanded. "What's at stake? I don't understand any of this. The man in the alley, the box, the phone call—what does it all mean?"

The man's smile faded, replaced by a look of something between pity and amusement. "You've been running from this your whole life, haven't you?" he asked, his tone almost soothing. "You've always known there was something more, something you were meant to do. But you've ignored it, buried it beneath everything else."

Meera's mind raced, her thoughts a jumbled mess. She had always known there was something different about her life, something that didn't quite fit. But was it really all tied to this? To this strange man and his cryptic words?

He stepped closer, his eyes never leaving hers. "You've seen the signs, haven't you?" he asked softly. "The whispers, the shadows that move just outside your vision, the things that don't quite add up. They've been there all along. And now, it's time to face them."

Meera shook her head, her heart pounding louder than ever. "I don't know what you're talking about," she whispered, her voice barely audible. "This... this isn't real."

The man's expression softened, almost sympathetically. "Oh, it's very real, Meera. And it's only just beginning."

He reached into his coat pocket and pulled out a small, gold pendant. It gleamed in the dim light, the intricate design of a serpent coiling around a gemstone catching her attention. He held it out to her, his eyes intense.

"Take it," he urged. "It's the first piece of the puzzle. The key to unlocking the truth you've been searching for."

Meera hesitated, her gaze shifting from the pendant to the man's eyes. Something in her gut told her that taking it would change everything. But it was already too late. Her fingers trembled as she reached out and accepted the pendant.

As soon as her skin touched the cold metal, a rush of visions flooded her mind—images of places she had never been, people she had never met, but who somehow felt familiar. And then, a single word echoed in her mind, repeating like a chant: *Choose.*

Part 3

The Reckoning Unfolds

Chapter 1

The Tides of Fate

The Calm before the Storm

Meera sat by the window, her gaze lost in the rhythmic sway of the trees outside. The morning light filtered through the branches, casting a peaceful glow across the room. Everything felt oddly still, as though the world itself was holding its breath, waiting for something that was yet to come.

The days since her encounter at the church had blurred together, each one heavier than the last. The mysterious man, his cryptic words, the pendant—all of it weighed on her mind. But it wasn't just the mystery of her past that gnawed at her. There was something darker, something lurking in the shadows of her present that threatened to overwhelm her.

She had hoped for some clarity, some sign that would help her make sense of it all. But instead, all she had was confusion. The weight of the unknown pressed down on her chest, leaving her feeling suffocated, trapped in a reality she couldn't control.

The truth, the man had said, would set her free, but it would cost her everything she knew.

What did that mean? What could it cost her? Meera had always believed that she was in control of her own destiny, that she could shape her own path. But now, it felt as though she was nothing more than a pawn in a game she didn't understand.

A knock on the door interrupted her thoughts, and she stood, her heart racing. Who could it be? Her apartment had been a sanctuary of solitude for the past few days, and the idea of someone else entering her space felt intrusive, unsettling.

She walked slowly to the door, each step heavier than the last. As she reached for the handle, a chill ran down her spine. She didn't know why, but she had a sinking feeling that the person on the other side was someone she wasn't prepared to face.

With a deep breath, she opened the door.

Standing in the hallway was a woman, tall and elegant, her dark hair pulled back into a tight bun. Her eyes were sharp, calculating, and she wore a dark green coat that contrasted sharply with the soft white of the apartment's walls.

"I'm sorry to intrude," the woman said, her voice smooth and confident. "But I need your help."

Meera felt her stomach tighten. Something about the woman's presence felt strange. "Help? Who are you?"

The woman smiled, but it didn't reach her eyes. "My name is Natasha. I'm here on behalf of someone who needs to speak with you."

A surge of fear coursed through Meera's veins. Who could this woman be working for? What did she want from her?

"Who sent you?" Meera demanded, her voice steady despite the unease bubbling within her.

The woman's gaze hardened. "I can't say. Not yet, anyway. But you'll want to come with me. This is bigger than you think."

Meera hesitated, her mind racing. Should she go with her? Or was this yet another trap in a long series of manipulations?

Before she could respond, Natasha stepped forward, her expression softening slightly. "You have no choice in this, Meera. Not anymore. Your fate has already been decided."

Whispers in the Dark

Meera couldn't shake the feeling that something was terribly wrong. The woman at her door, Natasha, had spoken with such authority, but there was a coldness in her eyes that made Meera question her intentions. She had always trusted her instincts, and right now, everything inside her screamed to run, to lock the door and forget this encounter ever happened.

But that wasn't an option, was it? Natasha had said it wasn't a choice—her fate had already been decided. The words echoed in her mind, unsettling and haunting, and as much as she wanted to deny them, a deeper part of her knew that she couldn't escape whatever had been set in motion.

With a final glance at the door, Meera reluctantly stepped out into the hallway. Natasha led the way, her heels clicking sharply on the floor as they descended the staircase in silence. Meera's heart thudded in her chest, and she couldn't help but wonder if she was walking into something far darker than she could comprehend.

The street outside was quiet, too quiet. The bustling city seemed a world away, and all that existed in the moment was the eerie calm that enveloped them. Meera's senses were heightened, every small sound, every shift of air, setting her on edge. She glanced around, but there was no one—no cars, no pedestrians—just an emptiness that made the hairs on the back of her neck stand up.

They walked in silence for what felt like an eternity before Natasha stopped in front of an unmarked door in an alleyway. The door was heavy, dark, and nondescript, much like everything else in this part of the city. Meera's stomach twisted in knots as she stared at it, the strange feeling of dread continuing to grow.

Natasha turned to face her, her expression unreadable. "This is it. We'll go in, and you'll finally understand everything."

What could that possibly mean?

Meera swallowed hard, trying to steady her racing heart. She had to know the truth. As terrifying as it all seemed, she had to understand what was happening. She nodded, her legs feeling heavy as she followed Natasha through the door.

Inside, the room was dimly lit, the air thick with the scent of old wood and something else—something metallic. The walls were lined with shelves, each one cluttered with objects that looked far too old to be of any practical use. Strange symbols and diagrams were scrawled across the walls, adding to the sense of unease that had settled deep within Meera's bones.

She glanced around, trying to make sense of her surroundings, but the more she looked, the more disoriented she felt. The room didn't make sense. It didn't belong in this world.

Natasha stood beside her, watching her every move. "Do you see it now?" she asked quietly. "Do you understand what's happening?"

Meera's throat went dry, her mind scrambling to make sense of the chaos before her. The walls, the symbols, the odd objects—they all seemed connected, but how? What did any of this have to do with her?

"You're part of something far bigger than you realize," Natasha continued. "It's all been planned, and now, there's no turning back. You have a role to play, whether you're ready for it or not."

Meera's pulse quickened. "A role? What are you talking about? I don't..."

Before she could finish, Natasha raised a hand to silence her. "You'll understand soon enough. For now, just listen. You need to know what's coming."

And with that, Natasha stepped back into the shadows, leaving Meera alone in the dimly lit room, surrounded by secrets that were too vast to comprehend.

The Truth beneath the Surface

Meera's head spun as she took in the eerie room around her. The walls seemed to close in, the cryptic symbols growing more suffocating with each passing second. She could hear her own breath, shallow and uneven, the pounding of her heart a constant reminder that nothing about this situation made sense. Everything felt wrong.

But Natasha's words hung in the air like a thick fog—*You're part of something far bigger than you realize.*

What could that even mean? How was she part of anything? She had spent most of her life trying to keep a low profile, staying out of trouble, focusing on her work. The quiet life she had built was suddenly shattered, replaced by shadows and secrets she wasn't prepared for.

"Why me?" Meera whispered, her voice trembling as she turned to Natasha, who stood silently in the corner, watching her with those cold, calculating eyes. "What am I supposed to do with all of this?"

Natasha didn't answer immediately. She moved to one of the shelves and began sifting through the clutter, her fingers brushing over old books and papers as if searching for something specific. Meera felt a rush of frustration building inside her. She had so many questions, and yet, Natasha seemed content to remain silent, lost in her own world.

Finally, Natasha spoke, her voice low and measured. "You've been chosen, Meera—chosen for your connection to this, to everything."

Meera's confusion deepened. She was chosen for what? What was she supposed to be connected to?

"Do you know who your father was?" Natasha asked, turning to face her with a look that seemed both expectant and calculating.

Meera blinked, stunned by the question. She had always known her father, of course—he had been a quiet man, distant but kind. He had passed away years ago, but his memory had always lingered, a quiet presence in her life. But what did he have to do with any of this?

"My father?" Meera repeated, struggling to find her voice. "He was a historian. There's nothing special."

Natasha shook her head. "Your father was part of something much greater—something that has been hidden from you, and from the world. He knew things that are only now beginning to resurface. And you, Meera, you are the key."

The weight of Natasha's words pressed down on Meera's chest, and she felt the room spin. The idea that her father had been involved in something secret, something powerful, was almost too much to process. She had no idea what Natasha was talking about, but the way she spoke—so sure, so certain—made Meera's blood run cold.

"I don't understand," Meera murmured. "What is all of this? What does it have to do with me?"

Natasha's eyes narrowed, and for a brief moment, she looked almost sorry. "It's not easy to understand, Meera. I know. But the truth is coming. And when it does, everything will change."

Meera wanted to scream, to demand answers, but something about Natasha's tone made her hold back. There was no escape from this, no running away. Whatever was happening was already in motion, and there was no stopping it.

"Tell me what I need to do," Meera whispered, resigned to whatever fate had been handed to her. She had no choice now but to follow this path, whatever it may bring.

Natasha studied her for a long moment before nodding. "The first step is simple. You have to trust me. You have to believe that what we're doing is for the greater good."

Meera felt a flicker of doubt. But deep down, she knew there was no turning back. She had to see this through, no matter the cost.

"Trust you?" Meera asked, her voice quiet. "How can I trust you when I don't even know what's going on?"

Natasha's lips curled into a faint, almost sad smile. "Because, Meera, you have no other choice."

The Storm on the Horizon

The days following her conversation with Natasha were a blur. Meera felt as though she had stepped into a world that was no longer her own, a world where every certainty she had ever known was now in question. Her quiet, predictable life was unraveling, thread by thread, and there was nothing she could do to stop it.

Her mind kept replaying Natasha's words—*You have no choice*—and with each repetition, the sense of helplessness grew. It felt like a storm was gathering on the horizon, slowly creeping closer, waiting for the moment to break. The weight of her father's hidden past, the cryptic symbols, the strange room—it all felt like the pieces of a puzzle that she could never quite fit together.

Despite the unease that had settled in her chest, Meera couldn't help but wonder about the truth behind Natasha's cryptic statements. She had been chosen, her father's past, the secrets in the room—what did it all mean? She had always been an ordinary woman, leading an ordinary life, and now, she was thrust into a reality that felt both too surreal and too dangerous.

Her phone buzzed on the table, breaking her from her thoughts. Meera glanced down and saw an unknown number on the screen. A sense of unease washed over her, but she answered anyway, feeling a knot of dread in her stomach.

"Hello?" she said, her voice tight with tension, trying to steady her breath.

"Meera, it's Natasha. I need you to come to me now."

The urgency in Natasha's voice sent a chill through Meera's body. She didn't want to go, didn't want to be dragged further into this world of secrets and danger, but something inside her told her that she had no choice. Every instinct in her was screaming to run, to lock herself away from the chaos, but her feet felt rooted to the ground.

"I don't know if I can trust you," Meera replied, her voice trembling. "What's going on? Why can't you just tell me everything?"

"Because you wouldn't believe me if I did," Natasha said, her tone sharp. "But you'll believe it when you see it. You're closer to the truth than you realize. And you need to understand what's at stake. It's bigger than anything you've ever known."

The line went silent for a moment, and Meera's pulse quickened. There was no going back now. She had to know the truth, no matter how terrifying it might be. The storm was coming—she could feel it.

"Alright," Meera said, swallowing her fear, trying to steady her racing heart. "Where do I meet you?"

After a brief pause, Natasha's voice returned, low and urgent. "I'll send you the address. Don't waste time. The storm is coming, Meera. And if you're not ready, it will swallow you whole."

The call ended abruptly, and Meera stood there, phone still in hand, her heart pounding in her chest. The storm was coming, and she had no idea how to prepare for it. But she knew one thing for sure—whatever came next, it was going to change everything.

The Beginning of the End

The city was cloaked in darkness by the time Meera arrived at the address Natasha had sent. The rain had started to fall in sheets, drenching her as she stood on the doorstep of an old building, its edges jagged and weathered. It was the kind of place that she never thought to enter, the kind of place that felt alive with secrets.

Her heart raced, her every instinct screaming at her to turn back, but she pushed forward. She had no choice now. Whatever lay ahead, there was no turning back. This wasn't just about her father's past anymore. It was about something far greater—something that, somehow, had everything to do with her.

She rang the doorbell, her finger trembling as she pressed the button. The sound echoed in the emptiness, a sharp contrast to the pounding of the rain. For a moment, there was no answer, and Meera felt the weight of the silence press down on her. Was she making a mistake?

The door creaked open slowly, revealing Natasha standing in the doorway, her expression unreadable. She motioned for Meera to enter, and without a word, Meera stepped inside.

The room was dimly lit, shadows dancing across the walls. A large wooden table sat in the center, covered with papers, maps, and old photographs. The air was thick with the smell of ink and dust, a strange mixture of the past and the present.

"Come in, Meera," Natasha said, her voice low and commanding. "You need to see this."

Meera hesitated for a moment, her eyes scanning the room. There was something about this place that made her feel like she was stepping into a different world—a world where the rules didn't apply, where danger lurked in every corner.

But she couldn't turn back now. Not when the answers were so close. She moved toward the table, her eyes falling on the scattered papers. There were symbols—ancient symbols she had never seen before—scribbled across the pages, some of them circled in red ink. Her breath caught in her throat as she recognized a few of them.

"These symbols... they're from the ancient texts, aren't they?" Meera whispered, her voice trembling.

Natasha nodded. "Yes. And your father knew more about them than anyone could have imagined."

Meera felt a chill run down her spine. Her father had never spoken of anything like this. He had always been a quiet man, content with his research and his books. But now, it seemed that everything he had ever kept hidden was slowly unraveling before her eyes.

"What does all of this mean?" Meera asked, her voice shaky as she reached for one of the photographs. It showed a group of men gathered around a large stone altar, their faces obscured by shadows. But there was one face she recognized—her father.

Natasha's eyes darkened as she looked at the photograph. "It means that your father was part of something much bigger than you could ever imagine. He was part of a secret society, Meera—a society that was dedicated to protecting the world from a power that could destroy everything."

Meera's mind reeled. A secret society? A power that could destroy the world? It was too much to take in. The questions were piling up faster than she could keep track of them, and the answers were slipping further out of reach.

"I don't understand," Meera whispered, shaking her head. "What was he protecting? And why didn't he ever tell me?"

Natasha stepped closer, her voice dropping to a whisper. "Because he knew the dangers of it. He knew that once you were involved, there would be no turning back. And he didn't want you to carry the burden of it."

The weight of Natasha's words sank deep into Meera's chest, making it hard to breathe. She had always believed that her father's life had been ordinary, that his death had been a simple, natural one. But now, everything she had known was being shattered.

"Why me?" Meera asked, her voice barely audible. "Why am I the one who has to be involved in this?"

"Because you're the only one who can stop it," Natasha said, her voice resolute. "You're the key, Meera. And if you don't act, everything we know will be lost."

Meera stared at Natasha, her mind spinning. She was in over her head, caught in a world that she didn't understand, filled with dangers that she couldn't even begin to comprehend. But as she looked at the woman standing before her, she realized that there was no choice. She had to face whatever came next. The storm was already here, and it was up to her to weather it.

Chapter 2

The Man Who Knew Her Name

The Unseen Visitor

The rain had stopped by the time Meera reached the unfamiliar part of the city, but the air was thick with the scent of wet earth, carrying a sense of foreboding with it. The lights from the streetlamps flickered intermittently, casting long shadows on the empty streets. The small alleyway she had entered felt like a world away from the bustling city she knew—a place forgotten by time.

Her heart thudded in her chest as she turned the corner. The building ahead was nondescript, its weathered stone walls marking the entrance to an apartment that seemed as much a mystery as the people who lived there. It was nothing like the places Meera had visited before. There were no signs, no names, just an air of quiet secrecy that seemed to hang in the air.

She hesitated, her fingers brushing the envelope in her bag. Inside, there was a single word written on a piece of paper: *Natasha*. No address, no instructions. Just a name. Meera had no idea what she was walking into, but the pull to know more was too strong to resist. And so, she had come, driven by a need to uncover the truth and unravel the enigma that her life had become.

As she stepped inside the building, the cold air rushed over her skin, making her shiver. The walls were lined with faded photographs, their edges curling, showing faces that were both familiar and strange. The faint sound of whispers seemed to echo from the shadows as she made her way down the hallway. A door at the end was slightly ajar, and Meera knew that beyond it lay the answers she had been searching for.

She knocked softly. There was no answer at first, and just as she began to think she had made a mistake, the door creaked open slowly. Meera's breath caught in her throat as a figure appeared in the doorway. It was a man, tall and broad-shouldered, with a face that was both reassuring and unsettling. His eyes locked onto hers with an intensity that made her heart race.

"You're late," the man said, his voice low and steady. There was no warmth in his tone, only a quiet expectation.

"I'm sorry," Meera stammered, feeling a surge of unease. "I..."

He interrupted her, stepping aside to let her in. "Come in. We don't have much time."

The room inside was dimly lit, with heavy curtains drawn over the windows. It felt like a room that had been preserved in time, untouched by the outside world. Meera stepped inside, her eyes scanning the space, trying to make sense of the objects scattered across the room. There were books piled high on a table, maps spread out on the floor, and old journals stacked neatly in the corner. The air was thick with the smell of aged paper and ink.

The man closed the door behind her, his gaze still fixed on her. "You're the one they sent, aren't you?" he asked, his voice cutting through the silence.

Meera nodded, unsure of what to say. "I don't understand. Who are you? What do you know about my father?"

The man's lips curled into a faint, knowing smile. "Your father was part of something much bigger than you could ever have imagined, Meera. And now, you've stepped into it."

Her heart skipped a beat. "What are you talking about?" she asked, the words feeling heavy on her tongue.

"The truth," he said, his gaze unwavering. "You're here because of the choices he made, and now it's your turn to make them. The question is: are you ready for what's coming next?"

The Unseen Voice

Meera stood frozen in place, her eyes never leaving the man before her. His presence seemed to fill the room, making it feel smaller, more intimate. Despite the dim lighting, his features were sharp, almost too sharp—every line on his face seemed carved from stone. His eyes, however, were what unsettled her the most. They were cold, distant, like the eyes of someone who had seen too much and had become numb to it all.

The silence stretched between them like a thick curtain, both of them seemingly waiting for the other to speak. Meera couldn't shake the feeling that she was in the presence of something or someone far beyond her comprehension.

"Who are you?" she finally asked, her voice barely above a whisper.

The man's lips twisted into a small smile, but it didn't reach his eyes. "I've been waiting for you, Meera," he said, his voice low and almost soothing. "You've come to ask questions. And I have answers. But whether you'll be able to handle them is another matter entirely."

Meera felt a shiver run down her spine. This wasn't a conversation she had expected to have. The man's words were cryptic, his tone measured, as though he were speaking from a place of knowledge that she couldn't even begin to fathom.

"I don't understand," she said, her frustration growing. "What do you mean? What do you know about my father? And why are you telling me all this?"

He took a step toward her, and for a moment, Meera felt as though the walls of the room were closing in. There was no escape now. She had crossed a line—one that had been drawn by forces far greater than anything she had ever known.

"I know everything about your father, Meera," he said, his voice growing more intense. "And I know about the path you're about to walk. Your father was one of the few people who understood the gravity of the situation, but he kept it hidden from you to protect you. Now, you must make your own choice. You must decide whether to follow the path he left behind, or to turn away and forget everything."

Meera took a step back, her mind reeling. "What are you talking about? What 'path'? And why me?"

The man's gaze softened, if only for a moment. "Because you're the key," he said, almost as if the words had slipped out unintentionally. "Your father knew it, and now, so do I. You're the one who can end this, Meera. But you'll have to be willing to make sacrifices. There's no turning back once you've crossed this threshold."

Meera's thoughts were a whirlwind of confusion and disbelief. She couldn't grasp what was happening, what this man was telling her. She had never asked for any of this. She had only wanted answers about her father, about the strange things that had been happening in her life. Now, she was being asked to make a decision that she didn't understand.

"Why didn't he tell me this?" she asked, her voice trembling. "Why didn't he trust me enough to tell me what was really going on?"

The man's expression hardened again, his eyes narrowing. "Because he knew you weren't ready. And now, you're still not. But you're here, and you can't walk away. Not anymore."

Meera swallowed hard, her throat dry. "What am I supposed to do?" she whispered.

The man didn't answer immediately. Instead, he walked toward a nearby table, his movements deliberate. He picked up a small, worn box and turned it over in his hands before placing it gently in front of her.

"This is yours," he said softly, pushing the box toward her. "It's a key to what comes next. But be warned—once you open it, there's no turning back."

Meera stared at the box, her heart pounding in her chest. Her instincts told her to refuse, to turn around and walk away from it all. But something inside her urged her to take it. She was already in too deep, and there was no turning back now.

Taking a deep breath, she reached out and picked up the box.

The Box of Secrets

The box felt strangely heavy in Meera's hands, as if it contained something more than just a physical object. She turned it over and over, examining every inch of its surface. It was old, worn with age, the wood smooth to the touch but cracked in several places. It seemed almost familiar. But how could it be? She had never seen it before, not in her life.

She glanced up at the man, who was watching her intently, his expression unreadable. "What's inside?" she asked, her voice barely above a whisper.

The man didn't answer at first. Instead, he walked to the window and stood there, staring out into the night. "You'll find out soon enough," he said, his voice distant, as though he were lost in thought. "But know this, Meera—what's inside the box isn't just for you. It's for everyone. Your father understood that. He made sure it was kept hidden, waiting for the right time."

Meera's mind was racing. She had so many questions, but none of them seemed to make sense in this moment. She had come here seeking answers about her father and the strange events happening to her, and now she was being handed a mysterious box with no explanation.

"I don't understand," she said, her frustration creeping into her voice. "What do you mean, it's for everyone? Why was it kept hidden? And why do I need to open it?"

The man turned to face her, his gaze steady and unwavering. "Your father was part of something much bigger than you realize," he said slowly. "He was involved in a secret that could change everything—everything you think you know about your world. And now, it's your turn to carry that burden."

Meera's breath caught in her throat. A secret? Something her father had kept hidden? What could it possibly be? She thought she knew him. He had always been distant, yes, but he had never seemed involved in anything dangerous.

"Burden?" she echoed, her voice shaking. "Why do you keep saying that? Why can't I just live my life like everyone else?"

The man took a step toward her, his eyes softening for the first time. "Because, Meera, the world is not what it seems. Your father knew that. And now, so do you. This box holds the key to everything—your future, the truth about your family, and what lies ahead. But to open it, you'll need more than just curiosity. You'll need to be prepared for what's inside."

The weight of his words hit her like a wave, and for a moment, Meera wondered if she had made a mistake by walking into this place, by trusting this man. But something inside her refused to back down. She had come too far to turn back now.

"I don't know if I'm ready," she admitted, her voice barely audible. "But I have to know. I have to understand."

The man nodded, as if he had expected her answer. "Good. But remember this, Meera: once you open that box, your life will never be the same. There's no going back. Are you willing to accept that?"

Meera didn't answer immediately. She stood there, holding the box in her hands, feeling the weight of its mystery, its significance. There was no turning back, she realized. She had already crossed the point of no return. Whatever was inside this box, whatever truth it held, was the key to unlocking the answers she had been searching for.

Taking a deep breath, she set the box down on the table and slowly, carefully, lifted the lid.

The Revelation

The box creaked open, and Meera's heart skipped a beat. Inside, nestled in a velvet lining, was a small, intricately carved pendant. It was shaped like an ancient key, its metal darkened with age but still gleaming faintly in the low light. She reached for it, her fingers trembling as she held it between them, examining its detailed design.

"Is this... is this what you were talking about?" Meera asked, her voice barely a whisper.

The man didn't immediately answer. Instead, he stepped closer, his eyes locked on the pendant. His expression, once unreadable, shifted slightly—almost imperceptibly—towards something deeper, something more guarded.

"That key," he said softly, "is the key to everything. It will lead you to the answers you seek, to the truth about your father's past. But be warned, Meera: what lies ahead is dangerous. It is a path few have survived. Your father knew that, which is why he kept it from you."

Meera felt a chill run down her spine. Her hand hovered over the pendant, her mind racing with questions. What was this key? What did it unlock? And why had her father kept it hidden for so long?

"You keep saying my father knew all of this," she said, her voice shaking with a mixture of confusion and anger. "Why didn't he tell me? Why did he keep it from me if I was supposed to know all of this?"

The man's gaze softened slightly, but there was a certain sadness in his eyes. "He loved you, Meera. That's why he kept it from you. He didn't want you to get involved in this. It's not a world for someone like you. But now that you're here, you have no choice. The key you hold is the gateway to a world your father spent his life protecting you from. It's the key to a mystery that's been unfolding for decades."

Meera's head spun. She had come here seeking answers about her father's death, about the strange events that had plagued her life. But this—this was something entirely different. She was standing on the precipice of a world she had never known, one that was filled with secrets, shadows, and dangers she couldn't begin to understand.

"What do I do with it?" Meera asked, holding the pendant in her hand, her fingers clenching around it. "What happens now?"

The man's expression hardened once again, his eyes narrowing. "You have to make a choice, Meera. The key will open the door to your father's legacy, but it will also bring you face-to-face with enemies who will stop at nothing to destroy you. You can't turn back now. The moment you opened that box, you stepped into a new reality. A reality where the rules are different, and the stakes are higher."

Meera felt her breath catch in her throat. The weight of the decision was almost too much to bear. She had always wanted answers about her father, but she had never imagined that they would lead her down this dark, dangerous path. She wanted to turn away, to forget about all of this. But deep down, she knew she couldn't. There was no turning back now.

"Tell me what I need to do," she said, her voice steady despite the turmoil inside her.

The man nodded, as if he had been expecting this. "You must go to the old library. There, you'll find the next piece of the puzzle. But be careful. You're not the only one looking for the truth. There are others—people who will do anything to stop you."

Meera's heart pounded in her chest. She had no idea what she was about to walk into, but she knew one thing for sure: her life was about to change forever.

The Path Forward

Meera stood still for a moment, the pendant in her hand a heavy reminder of everything that was at stake. The man's words echoed in her mind—*the next piece of the puzzle*—but what did that even mean? She had no idea what she was stepping into, but she couldn't deny the pull of something much bigger than herself. It was as if the world she had known had been ripped away, and now, she was faced with a truth she could no longer ignore.

The man seemed to sense her hesitation. He moved toward the door, his movements deliberate, purposeful. "The library," he said, his voice breaking through her thoughts. "It's not far. But time is of the essence, Meera. You don't have much. Trust no one."

"Trust no one," Meera repeated under her breath. The words felt like a weight in her chest. She had always believed that there were good people in the world—people who could be trusted. But now, it seemed like everything was upside down, and the rules were no longer what they seemed.

"You don't have to do this," the man said, his voice softening just a bit. "You can walk away now, forget about all of this. You don't have to know the truth. But if you choose to go forward, there's no going back. There are people who will want to use you, manipulate you. It's not a game, Meera. It's real."

She glanced at him, her heart racing. "And what about you? Who are you really?"

The man hesitated, and for the first time, Meera saw a flicker of uncertainty in his eyes. "I'm someone who has spent my life protecting the truth. But now, I'm afraid it's too late. The key you hold is part of a bigger plan, one that's been in motion for far longer than either of us."

Meera's mind raced. The puzzle pieces were scattered, but she couldn't yet make sense of the bigger picture. She didn't even know where to start, who to trust, or what to believe anymore. But she did know one thing: there was no turning back now. The path ahead was unclear, but she had already stepped onto it.

"I'll go," Meera said, her voice steady, though the uncertainty in her chest was palpable. "I'll find the library."

The man nodded, his face a mask of grim determination. "Good. But remember, Meera—this isn't just about finding the truth. It's about survival. You may have the key, but the ones you're up against have something more dangerous: power."

Meera looked down at the pendant again. It was small, inconspicuous, but it felt as though it carried the weight of the world in her palm. Whatever her father had been a part of, whatever legacy he had left behind, it was now her responsibility to carry it. She wasn't sure if she was ready, but she knew she had no choice.

The man moved toward the door, opening it to reveal the dark night outside. "Come. I'll take you to the library."

As she stepped into the cool air, Meera felt the weight of her decision settling on her shoulders. She didn't know what awaited her, but she couldn't walk away. There were too many questions, too many answers just beyond her reach. And now, she was closer than ever to finding them.

Chapter 3

Shadows behind the Curtain

The First Clue

Meera walked through the narrow alley, her eyes scanning the shadows. Every sound seemed amplified in the stillness of the night—the soft shuffle of her shoes against the cobblestones, the distant hum of traffic, the faint rustle of leaves in the trees overhead. But there was something else, something almost imperceptible, that made her skin prickle with unease. It was as if someone was watching her, just out of sight.

She quickened her pace, her fingers clutching the pendant around her neck. It felt heavier now, like it was pulling her toward something—something that was just out of reach. The man's words echoed in her mind: *Trust no one*. But who could she trust? She had no answers, no allies, only the cold, dark night and the feeling that the world around her was shifting in ways she didn't yet understand.

As she turned a corner, a figure emerged from the shadows. At first, Meera thought it was the man from the other night—the one who had given her the pendant—but as the figure stepped forward, she saw it was someone else entirely—a tall, broad-shouldered man with dark, piercing eyes. He didn't say anything at first, just watched her with an intensity that made her heart race.

Meera took a step back, instinctively reaching for the small knife tucked into the waistband of her jeans. She didn't know if it would help, but it made her feel a little safer. The man's gaze didn't waver, and for a moment, neither of them moved.

"Are you lost, Miss Sinha?" the man asked, his voice low and rough. His accent was unfamiliar, his words precise but lacking any warmth.

Meera's heart skipped a beat. How did he know her name? And why was he here, waiting for her?

"I don't know who you are," Meera stammered, her fingers still gripping the knife. "What do you want?"

The man's lips curled into a faint, almost imperceptible smile. "I don't want anything, Miss Sinha. I'm simply here to help you." He paused, his gaze never leaving hers. "But I'm afraid your path is much more dangerous than you realize. You've already made your first mistake by trusting the wrong people."

Meera's mind raced. Who was this man? How did he know about her? About the pendant? And why was he warning her?

Before she could respond, the man stepped back, disappearing into the shadows as quickly as he had appeared. Meera stood there for a long moment, the cool night air pressing against her skin. She didn't know what had just happened, but something in her gut told her that this was only the beginning.

She breathed deeply, her pulse still racing, and continued down the alley, but the sense of being watched only grew stronger. Every step felt like it was taking her deeper into a world of mystery she didn't understand. Was she truly ready for what lay ahead? What had her father left behind for her to uncover? She clutched the pendant once again, its weight now a reminder that she couldn't turn back.

It seemed that every decision she made pushed her further into a maze of shadows and half-truths, but there was no way out now. The key, her father's legacy, had already been set into motion.

The Stranger's Warning

The alley stretched before her, now an ominous tunnel in the dim light. Meera quickened her steps, the echo of her shoes on the cold stone reverberating in the air, amplifying the unsettling silence. She was no longer just walking. She was running from something she couldn't see, trying to outrun the shadows that seemed to cling to her with every turn.

The man's warning echoed in her ears: *Trust no one.* But who could she trust? Her father, who had kept so many secrets? The mysterious man with the pendant? Or the shadowy figure who had just crossed her path? It was all too much to digest.

As Meera neared the end of the alley, the streetlights flickered, casting long shadows that danced on the walls. A chill ran down her spine as she realized she wasn't alone. She stopped in her tracks, her senses heightened. She could hear a faint rustling behind her, the soft shuffle of feet on the ground. Someone was following her.

She turned quickly, her heart pounding in her chest. The alley behind her was empty. There was nothing but the soft glow of distant streetlights and the faint noise of the city beyond. Still, the hairs on the back of her neck stood on end. She wasn't sure if it was just her imagination, but something told her she wasn't alone in the dark.

With a deep breath, she continued walking, trying to push the fear to the back of her mind. But as she turned the corner, she noticed something strange—A piece of paper, crumpled and half hidden under a pile of leaves. Curiosity got the better of her, and she bent down to pick it up.

The paper was old, yellowed at the edges, and worn from handling. Meera unfolded it carefully, her fingers trembling slightly as she tried to make sense of the handwriting. The words were scrawled in a hurried, almost frantic script, as if the writer had been in a rush.

"The truth lies within the stones of the old temple. Seek what is hidden beneath the surface. Time is running out."

Meera stared at the paper, her mind racing. What temple? What stones? Who had left this message for her? The cryptic note seemed to be pointing her toward something, but it was all so vague. She was no closer to answers than she had been before, yet there was a sense of urgency growing within her. Something was coming, something she wasn't prepared for.

Before she could think further, a voice from behind broke her thoughts. "Looking for something?"

She whipped around, her heart leaping in her chest. It was the same man from the alley—the one who had warned her earlier. He stepped out of the shadows, his dark eyes gleaming with a strange intensity.

"I told you," he said in a low, measured tone, "your path is dangerous. You're already entangled in something much bigger than you realize."

Meera's mind raced. "What do you mean? Who are you?"

The man's expression softened slightly, but there was no warmth in it. "I'm someone who knows more about your father's past than you can imagine. And I'm here to make sure you don't get lost in it." He took a step closer, his gaze never leaving hers. "But time is running out, Miss Sinha. You need to hurry."

Before Meera could respond, he was gone, melting back into the shadows like a ghost. She stood there, staring at the spot where he had disappeared, the weight of the message pressing down on her. What was this all about? Why was she being dragged into a mystery that seemed so far beyond her control?

She looked down at the crumpled note again. The old temple, stones, beneath the surface—it was all too much to make sense of in the moment, but one thing was certain—she had no choice but to follow the trail, no matter where it led. Her father had left her something—something that was going to change everything. And Meera was determined to find out what it was.

Beneath the Surface

The rain had begun to fall by the time Meera reached the edge of the old temple grounds. Its rhythmic patter on the ground was a gentle but persistent reminder of the storm that was brewing not just in the skies, but also within her own heart. The note had led her here—*the truth lies within the stones of the old temple.* But what did that even mean?

The temple, long abandoned and forgotten by the city's hurried pace, stood in eerie silence. Its once-proud walls were crumbling, covered in ivy, and the air was thick with the scent of damp earth and decay. As she crossed the threshold, a chill ran down her spine. She had been to this place before, as a child, during the days when her father had brought her here for quiet walks. But it was different now. The temple felt alive, as though it had been waiting for her to return.

Meera's gaze moved to the large stone pillar near the center of the courtyard, the one her father had always admired. It seemed out of place, almost deliberately so—its smooth surface in stark contrast to the rough, weathered stones that made up the rest of the temple. Something about it drew her in. She couldn't explain why, but it felt like the key to everything.

Taking a deep breath, Meera stepped closer. The rain was falling harder now, but it only seemed to add to the atmosphere, as though nature itself were pressing her to continue. The stone pillar stood tall, untouched by time, almost regal in its quiet dignity.

Her fingers traced the surface of the pillar, feeling the coolness of the stone beneath her skin. She closed her eyes for a moment, trying to focus, to push away the overwhelming sense of urgency. The message had been clear—*beneath the surface*. But where exactly was this hidden truth she was supposed to uncover?

Then, she felt it. There was a faint indentation in the stone, hidden just beneath the layer of ivy. Meera's pulse quickened as she pressed her fingers into the indentation. The stone gave way, and with a low groan, a small section of the pillar slid open, revealing a hidden compartment.

Inside, there was a small, intricately carved box. Its surface was worn, but the carvings seemed to come alive under her touch, as though they were telling a story only she could understand.

She hesitated for a moment, the weight of the moment pressing on her. What was inside the box? Was it really her father's legacy? The truth he had promised to leave her? There was only one way to find out.

With trembling hands, Meera opened the box.

Inside was a scroll, old and yellowed with age. Carefully, she unrolled it, her eyes scanning the faded script. The writing was familiar, but the language was different—ancient, almost poetic. Meera's heart raced as she realized that this was a map—a map that would lead her to something far more significant than she could have imagined.

It wasn't just a map—it was a guide to a hidden place. The symbols on the paper seemed to be part of a puzzle, pieces that needed to be put together. The map was a puzzle in itself, but there was no mistaking its importance. This was the key to unlocking the truth, to finding out what had been hidden for so many years.

She folded the map carefully and tucked it into her coat, the weight of the secret now resting in her hands. It was clear that her journey had only just begun. But as she turned to leave the temple, Meera couldn't shake the feeling that someone was watching her—someone who had been waiting for her to uncover the truth. The shadows seemed to stretch around her, as if the darkness itself were closing in, and she couldn't help but feel that she was being drawn deeper into a web of secrets and danger that she could never escape.

The Echo of Secrets

Meera felt the weight of the hidden map in her coat pocket, its presence both reassuring and unsettling. It was as though the parchment was alive, pulsing with an energy that only she could feel. The more she thought about it, the more she realized just how much of her father's life she still didn't understand. This map—this guide to something hidden—was a key to unlocking the mysteries that had surrounded him for as long as she could remember.

As she walked out of the temple courtyard, her footsteps echoing in the silence, Meera couldn't help but feel the pull of the unknown. The city beyond the temple walls seemed like a distant memory, a world she no longer belonged to. She was no longer just Meera Sinha, the daughter of an influential businessman. She was now part of something bigger, something much darker.

The rain had stopped, but the air was thick with the scent of wet earth and the distant hum of the city. Meera walked down the narrow path that led back to the main road, but her thoughts were consumed by the map. She had to find the place it led to. She had to know what her father had left for her.

Suddenly, a voice interrupted her thoughts.

"You look like you've just uncovered a treasure, Miss Sinha."

Meera froze. She knew that voice. It was the same man from the alley, the one who had warned her earlier. His words were always cryptic, always veiled in mystery. But there was something else in his tone now—something that felt like a warning, as though he knew more than he was letting on.

She turned slowly, her hand instinctively reaching for the map in her coat pocket. The man stood in the shadows, his face obscured by the dim light of the streetlamps. But his presence was undeniable.

"What do you want?" Meera asked, her voice steady despite the unease creeping up her spine.

The man stepped forward, emerging from the darkness like a ghost. "I want to help you, Miss Sinha. But you have to trust me. The map you found—it's not the only thing you need. There's more, and you won't be able to piece it together alone."

Meera's heart raced. How did he know about the map? Had he been following her?

"You're wrong," she said, trying to hide the tremor in her voice. "I don't need your help. I can do this on my own."

The man's gaze softened, but his expression remained serious. "You don't understand. There are forces at play here that go far beyond your father's past. The secrets you're uncovering—they're not just about him. They go much deeper. You're playing with fire, Miss Sinha."

Meera took a step back, her instincts telling her to run, to get away from this man who seemed to know too much. But she also knew deep down that she couldn't ignore his warning. The more she uncovered, the more she realized that there were layers to this mystery she wasn't even close to understanding.

"What do you know about this?" Meera asked, her voice barely above a whisper.

The man hesitated before speaking again. "All I can tell you is that it won't be easy to find the truth you are seeking. And when you find it, you won't be able to unsee it. The world you know—it will never be the same again."

Meera swallowed hard, her mind racing. She wanted to argue, to push back against his words, but deep down, she knew he was right. There was no going back now. She had already stepped into a world that was filled with shadows and secrets, and there was no turning back. She had to follow this path, no matter the cost.

"Stay away from me," she said finally, her voice firm. "I don't need you, and I don't need your warnings."

With that, she turned and walked away, the echoes of his words still ringing in her ears. She didn't know if she was making the right choice, but she knew one thing for sure—this was her journey now. And she would uncover the truth, no matter where it led her.

Into the Abyss

Meera's heart raced as she left the temple grounds behind. The cool night air seemed to cut through her thoughts like a blade, her breath coming in shallow gasps as she processed everything that had just happened. The stranger's warning echoed in her mind, but it wasn't just his words that haunted her—it was the undeniable truth she had uncovered. The map, the hidden compartment in the stone pillar, her father's mysterious past—it was all connected. But to what end?

She glanced at the piece of parchment in her hand, its surface old and yellowed with age. The symbols and markings on the map were starting to make sense, but there was still so much she didn't understand. Her father had kept so many secrets, and now it was up to her to unlock them.

The streets were eerily quiet as she walked, the sound of her footsteps muffled by the soft drizzle of rain. The map burned a hole in her pocket, as though it were urging her to take action. But where? What was she supposed to do with it now?

A sudden thought hit her—*the man in the alley had said there was more.* But what did he mean? More of what? And who was he, really? Meera could feel the weight of her questions growing heavier with every step she took.

The alley where she had first seen the man seemed far behind now, but the unease in her chest didn't fade. There was something about that encounter that didn't sit right with her. His cryptic warnings, the way he seemed to know exactly what she was doing—he wasn't just some stranger. He knew things, things that were still hidden from her.

She shook her head, trying to push the thoughts away. She couldn't afford to get distracted. The map was the key to everything. She had to focus on it, follow its path, and uncover the truth her father had left for her.

She reached her apartment, the familiar sight of it bringing a sense of comfort that was quickly fading. Her mind was elsewhere, lost in the labyrinth of secrets and half-truths that seemed to be closing in around her. She needed a plan, something solid to hold onto, but there was nothing. Only more questions.

As she entered the building, she paused at the door to her apartment. The place felt different now, as if the very walls were holding their breath, waiting for her to make her next move. She stood there for a long moment, unsure of what to do next, before finally stepping inside.

The apartment was quiet—too quiet. Meera dropped her keys on the counter, her eyes scanning the room. The air felt thick with tension, as though something was out of place. She hesitated for a moment before walking further inside. The living room was empty, but there was something strange about the atmosphere. It felt colder than usual, the temperature having dropped without explanation.

Her gaze moved to the window, where the city lights flickered dimly in the distance. The night seemed to stretch on forever, the silence broken only by the faint hum of the city. As she turned to walk deeper into the apartment, a sudden noise made her freeze.

It was a soft sound, barely noticeable. But it was enough to send a shiver down her spine. Meera's hand instinctively reached for the map in her coat pocket. She stepped forward cautiously, her senses heightened.

The noise came again. This time, it was louder, more distinct. Meera's heart pounded in her chest as she realized that she wasn't alone.

The door to her bedroom was slightly ajar, the darkened interior visible from where she stood. Slowly, Meera moved toward it, her steps light and careful. She didn't know what awaited her inside, but she had a feeling that whatever it was, it was connected to the puzzle she was desperately trying to solve.

She reached for the door handle, her fingers trembling slightly as she turned it. The door creaked open, and there, in the center of the room, was a figure—a man.

But it wasn't just any man. It was the stranger—the one who had followed her, the one who had warned her.

And now, it seemed he had come to claim what was his.

Chapter 4

The Final Puzzle

The Silent Intruder

The morning light filtered softly through the blinds, casting long shadows across the room. Meera had barely slept. Her mind raced with thoughts of the stranger, the map, and the cryptic words he had left her with. There was a chill in the air, though it wasn't the kind that came with cold weather. It was the kind of chill that lingers in your bones, the kind that follows you long after the event that caused it.

She sat at her desk, the map spread out in front of her. The edges were frayed; the ink faded, but it still held the promise of something—something her father had hidden so carefully. But now it was more than just a map. It was the key to everything. The key to her past, her father's past, and perhaps even her future.

Meera couldn't ignore the feeling that she was being watched. It was subtle, like a presence at the edge of her vision, but it was there. She had checked the apartment several times, ensuring that everything was in place. There was no sign of forced entry, no indication that anyone had been inside. Yet, the feeling lingered, gnawing at her.

She reached for the map, her fingers brushing against the worn paper. It was strange how it seemed to hum with energy, as though it were alive. She spread it out fully, studying the markings, the symbols that had become so familiar to her. She had been over every detail a hundred times, but today something felt different. The patterns seemed to shift before her eyes, almost as if they were trying to tell her something.

A knock on the door broke her concentration. It was sharp, insistent.

Meera hesitated before rising from the desk. The feeling of being watched intensified, but she pushed it aside, telling herself it was just her imagination running wild. She walked to the door and opened it cautiously.

Standing in the doorway was a man—a familiar face, the stranger from the alley. But this time, he wasn't hiding in the shadows. This time, he was standing right there, looking her straight in the eyes.

"I told you we would meet again, Miss Sinha," he said, his voice low but confident.

Meera stepped back, instinctively reaching for the door to close it. But the man was quicker. He moved into the room, his presence filling the space like a storm rolling in.

"Who are you?" Meera demanded, her voice trembling despite her best efforts to stay calm. "Why are you following me?"

The man closed the door gently behind him, locking it with a soft click that made her stomach churn.

"You have questions," he said simply. "And I have answers. But not the ones you expect."

Meera's heart started beating faster. "What does that mean?" she asked, her mind racing.

The man smiled. It was a cold, unsettling smile that didn't reach his eyes. "It means that your father wasn't the man you think he was. And it also means that the map you've found is only the beginning. There's more—much more."

Meera felt a lump form in her throat. "More? What do you mean?"

The man's eyes never left hers. "There's a hidden truth—a truth about your father, about you, and about this city. The map is only a part of it. The rest is in the shadows."

Meera's mind reeled. She wanted to run, to scream, to demand answers. But something in the man's demeanor kept her rooted to the spot. He wasn't just a stranger anymore. He was part of something bigger, something she couldn't yet see.

"Why are you telling me this?" she asked, her voice barely above a whisper.

The man stepped closer, lowering his voice. "It is because you're not safe. There are people after you. They will stop at nothing to get what's yours. And if you don't act fast, it will be too late."

Meera's breath caught in her throat. She had always felt that there was more to her father's death, but now it seemed that she was on the edge of something far more dangerous than she could have imagined.

The man turned to leave, but before he did, he paused. "Remember," he said, his voice cold and final. "The truth is never what it seems. Be careful who you trust."

With that, he was gone.

The stranger was gone, but Meera stood there, frozen in place. She felt a wave of dizziness wash over her as the weight of his words settled in.

The truth was never what it seemed.

And now, she had to find out exactly what that truth was.

Behind Closed Doors

The sound of the door clicking shut behind him echoed in Meera's mind long after the man had left. She was alone again, standing in the middle of her apartment, but the space felt different now. It felt colder, as if the very air had shifted. She couldn't shake the feeling that something or someone was watching her.

Her hands trembled as she touched the map once again, the fragile paper pressing against her fingertips like a lifeline. The symbols and markings seemed to blur together, spinning in her mind, but she couldn't focus. The stranger's words lingered like a heavy fog.

"Your father wasn't the man you think he was..."

Meera repeated the words to herself, trying to make sense of them. The stranger had said the truth wasn't what it seemed, but how could she trust anything he said? He had appeared out of nowhere, offering cryptic warnings and half-truths. And yet, there was something undeniably compelling about him. Something that made her feel as though she had no choice but to listen.

She had always believed in the stories her mother had told her about his father—how he was a man of honor, of integrity, a man who fought for the truth. But now, with every passing moment, those beliefs were beginning to unravel. Was her father really the person she had thought him to be? What had he hidden from her?

Her thoughts were interrupted by a soft knock on the door.

Meera's heart skipped a beat. She wasn't expecting anyone. She moved cautiously toward the door, every instinct telling her to stay put. But she couldn't ignore the nagging feeling that someone was out there—someone who knew more than they were letting on.

She opened the door a crack, just enough to see who was on the other side. It was her neighbor, Mrs. Reddy, an older woman who lived in the apartment next door.

"Oh, Meera dear, I hope I'm not disturbing you," Mrs. Reddy said with a warm smile. "I just thought I'd check in on you. I've been hearing strange noises from your apartment lately. I was a little worried."

Meera felt a sudden pang of unease. Strange noises? She hadn't heard anything unusual, but then again, her mind had been preoccupied with everything that had been happening over the past few days.

"I'm fine, Mrs. Reddy," Meera said, forcing a smile. "Just a little tired, that's all. Thank you for checking in, but there's really no need to worry."

Mrs. Reddy's smile faltered for a moment, and Meera could have sworn she saw a flicker of doubt in her eyes.

"Well, if you're sure..." Mrs. Reddy said, her voice trailing off. "But if you ever need anything, don't hesitate to ask. We're neighbors, after all."

Meera nodded, but before she could say anything else, Mrs. Reddy turned and walked away, her steps echoing down the hallway. Meera stood in the doorway for a moment, watching her leave. There was something about that exchange that didn't sit right with her. Mrs. Reddy had seemed a little too interested in her well-being, as if she were probing for something. But what?

Meera closed the door and locked it behind her, her mind racing. She couldn't shake the feeling that she was being drawn into something far bigger than herself. Someone knew what she was doing, and someone was watching her every move.

She glanced at the map again, trying to focus. There had to be something she was missing. The symbols, the markings—they all had to mean something. She had to uncover the truth, no matter what it cost her.

But as she studied the map, another thought crossed her mind. What if she wasn't the only one looking for answers? What if someone else had already found the truth—and was now coming for her?

The Shadow in the Alley

The city was alive with movement. People hustled through the streets, absorbed in their own worlds, unaware of the storm quietly brewing beneath the surface. Meera walked briskly down the narrow alley, her thoughts consumed by the stranger's visit and the cryptic message he had left her with. The weight of his words pressed heavily on her chest, making it hard to breathe.

The alley was dimly lit, shadows stretching across the cracked pavement like dark fingers reaching out to touch her. Meera felt a chill run down her spine as she glanced around, but there was no sign of danger. The world seemed normal and ordinary, yet she knew that everything had changed.

She paused at the end of the alley, her hand gripping the edge of the map in her pocket. The map was the key to everything. Her fingers brushed against the crumpled paper, and for a brief moment, she imagined the truth unfolding before her. Her father's secrets, hidden away for so long, were slowly coming to light.

But then, something caught her eye. It was a figure—a shadow.

It was fleeting, just a flicker in the corner of her vision. She turned sharply, her heart racing, but the alley was empty. Her breath came in short, uneven gasps. Had she imagined it? Or was someone following her?

She scanned the street, but no one seemed to be paying her any attention. It was just another busy evening in the city. But the feeling of being watched, of being hunted, lingered like a dark cloud hanging over her.

Meera took a deep breath and forced herself to keep moving. She couldn't afford to let fear control her. The map, the mystery—it was all connected. And she wasn't about to back down now.

But as she reached the end of the alley, a voice echoed from behind her. It was low, calm. Almost like a whisper on the wind.

"Looking for something, Miss Sinha?"

Meera froze. The voice was familiar, but it wasn't the stranger from before. It was someone else. Someone she didn't recognize, but who seemed to know exactly who she was.

She spun around, her eyes searching the darkness, but there was no one there—just shadows and the sound of her own heartbeat pounding in her ears.

The voice came again, closer this time.

"I know what you're after," the voice said, tinged with a hint of amusement. "And I know you'll never find it. Not unless you're willing to pay the price."

Meera's throat went dry. She couldn't move, couldn't think. The words felt like a trap, a warning, but she didn't know who was speaking or what they wanted.

Then, from the shadows, a figure stepped forward.

A man, tall and lean, dressed in a dark suit. His face was obscured by a hat, but his eyes shone with an eerie, unsettling intensity. He was the one who had spoken.

"Who are you?" Meera demanded, her voice shaking.

The man smiled, a cold, calculating smile. "I'm the one who's been keeping an eye on you. I'm the one who's been waiting for you to come to me."

Meera's mind raced. She didn't have time for this. She needed to find answers, not get caught up in some twisted game of cat and mouse.

"I don't have time for your games," she said firmly, taking a step back. "Tell me who you are and what you want."

The man tilted his head slightly, his smile never wavering. "What I want is simple," he said, his voice almost too calm. "I want what's mine. And I'm willing to do whatever it takes to get it."

Meera's heart skipped a beat. "What's yours?" she whispered, barely able to breathe.

The man's eyes narrowed. "The map, Miss Sinha. You know exactly what I'm talking about."

Meera felt a sudden wave of panic wash over her. She had known this day would come, the day when someone would finally come looking for the map. But she hadn't expected it to happen like this, not in the middle of the city, in the dead of night.

"Why do you want it?" she asked, her voice barely a whisper.

The man stepped closer, his presence looming over her. "It is because I've been searching for it for years. And now, I'm finally going to get what I deserve."

Meera swallowed hard, her mind racing for a way out. She had to act fast. She couldn't let this man get his hands on the map. It was too important. But how could she escape him? How could she fight back?

Before she could decide, the man took a step forward, his hand reaching out to grab her arm.

"Give it to me," he demanded.

Meera's pulse raced as she jerked away, but the man was too quick. His grip tightened, pulling her closer.

"I said, give it to me!" he repeated, his voice laced with menace.

The Price of Secrets

Meera's heart raced as the man's cold grip tightened around her wrist. The alley felt narrower, the shadows deeper. The city around her, once full of life, now seemed distant and unimportant. Everything had shifted the moment the man had spoken. His words, laced with menace, seemed to echo in her mind.

"I told you, I want the map," the man hissed, his breath hot against her ear. "And I'll do whatever it takes to get it."

Meera twisted her wrist, trying to break free, but his hand was like iron. Her mind raced, trying to find a way out. She couldn't let him get the map, not now. It was too dangerous, too vital. But she was trapped—there was no one in sight, no one to help her.

"Please," she gasped, trying to steady her breath. "You don't understand. I don't even know what it is you want. I'm just trying to..."

"Shut up," the man interrupted sharply. "You think I'm going to listen to your lies? I've been watching you for weeks. I know exactly what you have. And I know that if I don't get it now, I'll never get another chance."

His words were a dagger in her chest. He was right—she had known this moment was coming, but she hadn't prepared for it. She hadn't been ready for someone like him.

The man's grip slackened slightly as he noticed the flicker of fear in her eyes. But the moment of respite was short-lived. He yanked her forward, dragging her down the alley.

"Stop!" Meera screamed, her voice breaking through the stillness of the night. But the sound seemed to be swallowed by the darkness, leaving her feeling small and helpless.

The man's grip remained firm, but his expression softened just a fraction. "You're not going to get away, Miss Sinha. You can't outrun me. No one can. Not when I have everything I need."

Meera's thoughts were racing. She couldn't outrun him; that much was true. But there had to be another way out. She had always been resourceful, always found a way to turn the tables when cornered.

Then it hit her.

She had something—a weapon, one she had carried for years, tucked away in the inner pocket of her coat. It wasn't much, but it might be enough to give her a fighting chance.

The man pulled her closer, his face inches from hers. He smiled again, that cold, predatory smile that made her skin crawl. "You're not going anywhere, Miss Sinha. You're in my world now."

But before he could say anything else, Meera's hand shot up, grabbing for the small object hidden beneath her coat. She pulled it out—a sharp, sleek knife, its silver blade gleaming under the dim streetlights.

The man froze for a moment, his eyes narrowing as he saw what she held. He stepped back, momentarily wary of the weapon in her hand. "You think you can fight me with that?" he sneered. "You're just a girl. What do you think you're going to do?"

Meera's heart pounded in her chest, but her resolve hardened. She wasn't just a girl. She was Meera Sinha, and she wasn't going to let anyone take what was hers—not without a fight.

"I don't care who you are," she said, her voice low but steady. "I'll do whatever it takes to protect myself."

The man's gaze flickered to the knife, and for a moment, he hesitated but only for a moment.

"You think you can stop me?" he said, his voice dripping with amusement. "You really think you can stop me from getting what I want?"

Without warning, he lunged forward again, faster than Meera had anticipated. But she was ready. With a swift motion, she thrust the knife in his direction, catching him off guard. The blade scraped against his coat, missing him by inches.

He let out a growl of frustration and lunged again, but this time, Meera was ready. She sidestepped, her feet moving with practiced precision, and in one fluid motion, she slammed the knife into his side.

He staggered back, his eyes wide with shock. For a moment, it seemed like the world had frozen. The man stood there, breathing heavily, his hand clutching at his side as blood stained his fingers.

"You're going to regret this," he hissed through gritted teeth. "This isn't over, Miss Sinha. You've made a powerful enemy tonight."

But Meera didn't wait to hear any more. She turned and ran, the sound of his voice fading as she disappeared into the night, her heart still pounding in her chest.

The Last Chance

Meera's breath came in sharp gasps as she turned a corner, her feet pounding against the pavement. The alley she had just escaped from seemed to stretch endlessly, each shadow and crevice mocking her sense of safety. The adrenaline surged through her veins, but so did the fear—fear of being followed, of making the wrong move, of the consequences if she failed.

She could hear the man's footsteps behind her, growing fainter by the second, but she wasn't going to stop running until she was absolutely sure she was safe.

Her thoughts, however, were a mess. Her mind kept flashing back to the moment she had stabbed him, to the shock in his eyes, and to the pain in her chest. She had acted out of instinct—survived on instinct—but the moment she made that choice, everything had changed.

She had always known this day might come, but she hadn't expected it to be so soon. The stakes were higher now, and the weight of the secret she carried seemed to crush her at every turn. The map, the one thing that had caused all of this chaos, was still safe—for now.

Meera's hand instinctively went to her coat pocket, where the map was hidden. She could feel the familiar shape of it, the edges pressed against her palm, and for a fleeting moment, a sense of relief washed over her. But it was short-lived. She knew the man wouldn't stop. He couldn't afford to. Not when the prize was so close.

She didn't know how much longer she could keep running. Her body was tired, her legs aching with each step, but her mind was sharper than ever. She couldn't let him catch her, not now, not when she was so close to discovering the truth about the map.

Just as she rounded another corner, she felt a tug at her sleeve. Her instincts kicked in before her mind could process what was happening. She spun around, pulling out the knife she had used earlier, but stopped just in time.

There, standing before her, was a woman. She was tall, dressed in dark clothing that blended perfectly with the night. Her eyes, however, were the most striking part—pale blue, like a stormy sea.

"Meera," the woman said softly, her voice carrying an air of authority. "I've been looking for you."

Meera narrowed her eyes, taking a step back. "Who are you?"

The woman didn't answer directly. Instead, she simply said, "You're in danger. More than you realize. And if you don't come with me now, you'll never make it out alive."

Meera's heart skipped a beat. She had never seen this woman before, but the fear in the woman's eyes was enough to make her hesitate.

"Why should I trust you?" Meera demanded, gripping the knife tighter, her fingers trembling.

"I understand your doubt," the woman replied, holding up her hands in a gesture of peace. "But time is running out. The man who's chasing you is more dangerous than you know. You need to leave this city, and you need to do it now."

Meera's mind raced. This was the last thing she needed—another person trying to get her to do something. She had enough on her plate as it was. But the woman's words rang true. She had felt the danger closing in ever since the moment the man had found her.

"Who are you really?" Meera asked again, her voice low but urgent.

The woman's lips curled into a slight smile, and for a brief moment, Meera saw something familiar in her expression—something that felt oddly like trust.

"You don't have to trust me," the woman said. "But you will soon enough. Right now, we don't have time for questions. The answers will come, but only if you choose to come with me."

Meera glanced around, her instincts still telling her to run. But something about the woman's presence, the calm in her voice, made her hesitate.

In that moment, as the sound of footsteps grew nearer, Meera knew she didn't have a choice. She made up her mind and, lowering the knife, said, "Alright, let's go."

The woman gave a curt nod and led the way down another narrow alley, disappearing into the shadows.

Part 4

The Final Truth

Chapter 1

The Hidden Path

The Echoes of Yesterday

Meera stood at the threshold of the ancient temple, her heart beating loudly in her chest. The morning sun had just begun to rise, casting a soft golden hue across the landscape. The air was thick with the scents of incense and jasmine, but an underlying tension hung in the air.

For weeks now, she had been on the run—always one step ahead of those who wanted to silence her, always chasing something elusive, something she couldn't yet name. The map, the one that had once been her only hope, had become a burden, a curse that had brought nothing but chaos. But now, standing here, at the heart of this sacred place, Meera felt an overwhelming sense of clarity.

She was not just running anymore. She was on the brink of something much bigger—something that could change everything. This temple, ancient as it was, held the key to the truth she had been searching for.

The stone walls were covered in intricate carvings, each telling a story of forgotten gods and lost civilizations. Meera's fingers traced the symbols, the cool stone soothing her as she tried to make sense of it all. What was the connection between the temple and the map? How did they fit together?

A voice broke through her thoughts, low and calm. "You've come far, Meera. But your journey is far from over."

Startled, Meera turned quickly, her hand instinctively going to her side, where the knife rested.

Standing before her was a man—tall, with an air of quiet authority. His face was obscured by the shadows, but his presence felt undeniable.

"Who are you?" Meera demanded, her voice steady despite the pounding in her chest. "And how do you know my name?"

The man took a step forward, his eyes piercing in their intensity. "I know you better than you think. The question is: do you know yourself?"

Meera narrowed her eyes, scanning his face for any hint of recognition. "I don't have time for riddles."

The man smiled, though it was more of a knowing curve of his lips. "Then let me be clear. You are standing at the crossroads of your destiny. The map, the secrets you seek—they are all part of a larger plan. And you, Meera, are at the center of it."

The weight of his words hit her like a wave, and for the first time in weeks, Meera allowed herself to feel something other than fear—curiosity. What was he talking about? How could she be the center of something so much larger than herself?

Before she could speak, the man continued, "The truth you seek lies not in the map alone, but in the journey you must undertake. There are forces at work, forces beyond your understanding. But you have something they want, something you don't yet fully comprehend."

Meera's thoughts raced. What could she possibly have that was so important? She had nothing but the map and a life full of questions. But even as she thought this, a part of her knew that the man was right. This was bigger than just the map. It was bigger than her.

"Why are you telling me this?" Meera asked, her voice laced with both suspicion and intrigue.

The man's gaze softened, and for a moment, he seemed almost compassionate. "It is because your choices will determine the future of us all. You are the key, Meera. But first, you must understand the path you are on."

Meera felt a chill run down her spine. The path she was on? She had been running for so long, so desperately trying to stay one step ahead. She had never once stopped to think about the bigger picture.

"You've come to the right place," the man said, his voice low. "But now, you must take the next step—toward the truth. Follow me."

Without waiting for her response, he turned and began walking toward the temple's inner sanctum.

Meera hesitated. Everything in her told her to trust him, to follow him. But doubts lingered. Was this just another trick? Another trap designed to keep her running in circles? Yet, despite her fear, she couldn't shake the feeling that this was the moment she had been waiting for.

With a deep breath, Meera followed.

The Path Ahead

Meera's footsteps echoed softly in the stone corridor, the cool, damp air pressing against her skin. The man led her deeper into the temple, past ornate statues and carvings that seemed to tell stories of gods and demons long forgotten. It felt as though the walls themselves whispered ancient secrets, their voices carried through the centuries.

She tried to steady her thoughts, but everything felt overwhelming. The stranger had said she was the key, but what did that mean? What truth could she possibly hold? She had been running her entire life, never feeling like she belonged anywhere. Her journey had always been one of survival, of barely keeping ahead of those who pursued her. She never thought she was anything special. But now, standing here, in this sacred place, she couldn't shake the feeling that everything was about to change.

The man stopped before a large stone door, adorned with intricate symbols. It looked like it had been untouched for centuries. He turned to her, his expression unreadable.

"Behind this door," he said, his voice calm and unwavering, "lies the truth you've been searching for. But remember, Meera, the journey does not end here. This is only the beginning."

Meera nodded, feeling a mixture of fear and anticipation. She had come so far, but now that the moment was here, she wasn't sure she was ready. What if the truth was more than she could handle? What if everything she had believed in was a lie?

The man reached for a hidden lever beside the door, and with a low rumble, the massive stone door began to open, revealing a dark, musty chamber beyond. The air felt heavy, as if the room itself was holding its breath, waiting for her to step inside.

He stepped aside, gesturing for her to enter. "This is your journey now, Meera. No one can walk it for you."

Meera hesitated for only a moment before stepping through the threshold, her heart pounding in her chest. The room was vast, filled with stone pillars and old tapestries hanging from the walls, their colors faded with time. In the center of the room stood a large pedestal, on top of which rested a small, ancient box.

It looked harmless, yet Meera knew instinctively that whatever was inside it held the answers she had been seeking for so long. But what if opening it would change everything? What if it brought even more danger into her life?

"Take it," the man said, his voice echoing through the chamber. "It is yours to open. But remember, the choice is always yours."

Meera slowly approached the pedestal, her fingers trembling as she reached out for the box. It was cold to the touch, the metal smooth and unyielding. She took a deep breath, gathering her courage. This was it. The moment she had been waiting for. She had come so far, and there was no turning back now.

With a steady hand, she lifted the lid.

Inside the box, nestled in velvet, was a small, intricately carved key. Its shape was unlike anything Meera had ever seen before. It seemed to shimmer with an otherworldly glow, as though it held a power all its own.

She picked it up carefully, the weight of it strange in her palm.

"The key to the truth," the man said softly, as if reading her thoughts. "But it is not just a key to a door. It is the key to understanding everything that has brought you here. The journey is yours to make, but this key will guide you."

Meera held the key tightly, feeling the weight of her choices. There was no turning back now. The truth was within her grasp, but the path ahead was still uncertain.

"Thank you," she whispered, her voice barely audible. "I don't know what to do with it, but I'll find my way."

The man nodded. "You already have, Meera. Your journey has always been about understanding the truth within yourself. This key is simply a reminder of that. Now go, the road ahead awaits."

Meera turned and left the chamber, the key clutched tightly in her hand. She had taken the first step toward the truth, but she knew the journey would only become more difficult from here. She didn't know where the key would lead her, but for the first time in a long while, she felt ready to face whatever lay ahead.

The Truth Unfolds

Meera's footsteps faltered as she left the chamber, the key still burning in her hand. Her heart was racing, her thoughts a tangled mess of questions and fears. She had always been searching for something—some way to make sense of the chaos in her life, to understand why she was always running, always hiding. But now, with the key in her hand, the reality of it all felt almost unbearable.

She paused in the corridor, feeling the weight of what she had just uncovered. It was as if a veil had been lifted, and for the first time, she could see clearly. But what did it mean? What was the truth she had uncovered? And what did she have to do with it?

"Meera..." The soft voice came from behind her, making her spin around. The man was standing just outside the doorway, his eyes filled with an intensity she couldn't quite place.

"The key," he said, nodding toward the small object in her hand. "It is a symbol of much more than what you see. It holds the power to unlock the doors of your past, to reveal what has been hidden from you."

Meera swallowed hard. She had tried so hard to forget the past, to bury it deep within herself. The memories of her family, her childhood, and the things that had happened to her—it was all too painful to face. But now, with the key in her hand, it felt like she had no choice. The door to her past was about to be opened.

"I'm not ready," she said, her voice shaking slightly. "I don't know if I can handle what's behind it."

The man studied her for a long moment, his gaze unwavering. "No one is ever truly ready, Meera. The truth has a way of finding us when we least expect it. But the choice to face it, to accept it, is yours. And it is yours alone."

He turned and began to walk down the corridor, his steps measured, as if he were certain of something Meera could not yet comprehend. She followed him instinctively, her feet moving almost on their own.

"Do you believe in fate?" he asked after a long silence, his voice soft and contemplative.

Meera didn't answer immediately. She wasn't sure what she believed anymore. Fate, destiny—those words had always felt like empty concepts to her. She had never believed that things happened for a reason, that there was some grand design behind everything. Life had always been random, unpredictable, and full of struggle.

But now, holding the key, standing in this ancient temple, surrounded by mystery and secrets, she couldn't help but feel that something was at play—something beyond her understanding.

"I don't know," she finally said, her voice quiet. "Maybe. But I don't know what to believe anymore."

The man smiled faintly, as though he understood more than she did. "You'll find your answer in time," he said. "The key you hold is a bridge between your past and your future. The truth is waiting for you to claim it."

Meera looked down at the key, her fingers tightening around it. The path ahead was uncertain, and part of her wanted to run, to hide again. But deep inside, she knew there was no going back. She had already taken the first step, and the road before her was one she would have to walk.

The man paused in front of a small door, his hand resting on the handle. "This is where it begins," he said, his voice filled with reverence. "But only you can decide how it ends."

Meera's breath caught in her throat. She could feel the weight of the moment pressing down on her, the significance of everything that was happening. Her journey had led her here, to this very moment, and she could not escape it.

With a steady hand, she reached for the door, the key still clutched tightly in her fingers. As she turned the handle, she felt a rush of emotions—fear, anticipation, uncertainty. But above all, there was a sense of purpose. She had come this far, and she wasn't about to turn back now.

The door creaked open, and she stepped inside, the key in her hand now feeling like more than just an object. It was a symbol of everything she had been searching for, and everything she had to face.

As the door closed softly behind her, Meera felt a strange sense of peace wash over her. She had taken the first step toward the truth. And no matter what awaited her inside, she was ready to face it.

The Unravelling Threads

Meera stood at the threshold of the darkened room, the key still warm in her palm, as though it were pulsing with its own life. The door in front of her was ancient, its wood darkened with age, etched with symbols she couldn't decipher. But the energy in the air was unmistakable. This was the moment—the moment when everything she had ever known would either collapse or be revealed in its truest form.

She took a deep breath, steadying herself. There was no turning back. This was the beginning of something far bigger than she had ever imagined. Her fingers tightened around the key, and with a swift motion, she turned it in the lock.

The door creaked open, revealing a small, dimly lit chamber. The air inside was heavy with dust, and the silence was deafening. Meera hesitated for a moment, and then stepped inside. The room was barren except for an old, worn wooden chest sitting in the center. It was covered in intricate carvings, symbols that seemed familiar but alien at the same time. She could feel the weight of the chest, as though it held the answers to every question that had ever plagued her.

Slowly, she approached the chest, her heart pounding in her chest. With trembling hands, she knelt down and lifted the lid. Inside, there were several items—old papers, a few small trinkets, and what looked like an ancient journal. Meera's eyes went immediately to the journal. It was bound in leather, the edges frayed with time, its surface etched with the same symbols as the chest.

Her breath caught in her throat. This was it. The answers she had been searching for were right here, waiting for her to find them. She reached for the journal, but as her fingers brushed the cover, a sharp chill ran down her spine. It was as though the room itself had shifted, as though the very air around her had thickened with the weight of something unspeakable.

With a sense of urgency, she flipped the journal open, scanning the first page. It was filled with elegant, looping handwriting—familiar, yet foreign. The words seemed to dance before her eyes, as if beckoning her to understand, to decode what had been written. She tried her best, but she couldn't make sense of the cryptic passages. They were written in a language she had never seen before, their meaning lost in time.

Frustration and fear bubbled up inside her. This wasn't what she had expected. She had hoped for clear answers, for a way to make sense of her past. But instead, she was left with more questions. And with those questions came an overwhelming sense of dread, a feeling that she was being drawn into something far darker than she had anticipated.

She slammed the journal shut, feeling the weight of the moment crash down on her. What had she uncovered? What was she meant to do with this?

As she sat there, trying to collect her thoughts, she felt a presence behind her. The air shifted once more, and she turned, her heart hammering in her chest. The man—the one who had guided her thus far—stood in the doorway, his face unreadable. His eyes held a depth of understanding that made her skin prickle.

"Don't be afraid," he said softly, his voice like a calm breeze. "The answers are here, Meera. You just have to look deeper."

She stood up, her knees trembling slightly, and walked toward him, the journal still clutched tightly in her hands. She couldn't explain it, but something in his presence seemed to offer her comfort, even as her mind raced with fear and confusion.

"Who are you?" Meera asked, her voice barely a whisper. "Why are you helping me?"

The man's gaze softened, and for the first time, she saw a flicker of emotion in his eyes. "I am someone who has walked the path you are about to tread. You are not the first to seek the truth, and you will not be the last. But the journey you're on is yours alone."

His words hung in the air between them, heavy with meaning. Meera felt a pang in her chest. She had always thought she was alone in her struggle, that no one else could understand her pain. But now, standing before this man, she realized that she wasn't alone. There were others who had walked this path before her—and there would be others who would follow.

"What happens now?" she asked, her voice breaking slightly as she clutched the journal to her chest.

"Now," the man said, his voice steady, "you must make a choice. You can choose to turn away from the truth, to close the door and walk away. Or you can choose to face it, to embrace the past and the future that lies ahead."

Meera took a deep breath, looking down at the journal. Her fingers trembled as she traced the worn edges. She knew what she had to do. There was no turning back now. The truth was here, within her grasp. And whatever it held, she would face it—head-on.

With newfound resolve, Meera nodded. "I'm ready."

The man smiled, a faint, approving smile. "Then let's begin."

The Reckoning Begins

Meera's mind was a whirlwind of thoughts, each one spiraling faster than the last. She had made her choice. She had embraced the truth, whatever it might bring. But there was no turning back now. The room was charged with an energy she couldn't comprehend, an invisible force pressing down on her chest. She had come so far, yet the real test was just beginning.

The man stood in front of her, his calm demeanor never faltering. He seemed to understand her turmoil without saying a word. His presence was like a silent anchor, holding her steady as the storm of her thoughts raged on inside her.

"You've chosen, Meera," he said softly, his voice steady yet filled with a weight that seemed to echo in her soul. "Now you must face what comes next. The path ahead is not easy. It will test you in ways you cannot yet imagine."

Meera nodded, her throat tight as she struggled to hold back tears. She had never felt so vulnerable, so exposed. The journey she had embarked on had already shaken the very foundations of her life. And now, it was only just beginning.

"What do I need to do?" she asked, her voice barely above a whisper. Her gaze dropped to the journal she still clutched in her hands, the pages seeming to pulse with energy. There was more to it, and she could feel it. But what?

The man gave a small, knowing smile. "You must open it, Meera. Open the journal. Let it reveal its secrets."

Her fingers trembled as she flipped open the cover of the journal, the soft creak of the leather filling the room. The air seemed to thicken, the weight of the moment pressing down on her shoulders. She didn't know what she was expecting—answers, perhaps, or maybe the truth of her past. But what lay on those pages was more than she could have ever imagined.

As she scanned the pages, a strange sensation washed over her. The words began to blur, shift, and change. The ink seemed to dance before her eyes, forming shapes, symbols, and images that were not of this world. It was as though the journal itself was alive, responding to her touch.

Her heart raced as she tried to make sense of the chaos in front of her. And then, as if by some unspoken force, the symbols on the pages began to form a picture—a map that led her to a place she had only heard of in whispers—the temple.

It was a place of great power, a sacred site that had been lost to time. Legends spoke of its existence, but no one had ever been able to find it. Meera had always dismissed those stories as mere myths. But now, with the map before her, she realized the truth.

The temple was real.

And it was her destiny to find it.

"The temple," she whispered, her voice breaking through the silence of the room. "It's real. It's all real."

The man stepped closer, his gaze steady. "Yes. It is real. And now, you must go to it. You must unlock the final secret."

Meera's mind raced. She had thought she was ready, but this? This was beyond anything she had imagined. What did it mean? What was the secret she was meant to unlock? And why her? Why was she the one chosen for this task?

But as she looked at the map again, she felt something deep within her stir—a connection, a sense of purpose she had never known before. This was it. This was her path. And no matter how daunting it seemed, she knew she had to follow it.

"Will I be alone?" Meera asked, her voice filled with uncertainty.

The man nodded slowly. "You may feel alone, but you are never truly alone. The temple will guide you. The path will reveal itself, step by step. All you must do is trust in what you know. Trust in yourself."

Meera swallowed hard, the weight of his words sinking in. The uncertainty still clung to her, but she knew what she had to do. She had to go. She had to find the temple, uncover its secrets, and face whatever awaited her there.

With a final look at the journal, Meera closed it gently and stood up. Her heart was still racing, but there was a new sense of clarity in her chest. She wasn't alone. She had a purpose. And the journey ahead was hers to take.

The man gave her one last, approving nod. "It is time, Meera. Your journey begins now."

Chapter 2

The Temple of Forgotten Secrets

The First Step

Meera stood on the threshold of an unknown journey, her heart pounding in her chest. The map in her hand seemed to hum with an energy that was almost palpable, as though it were alive. The faint glow of the setting sun bathed her in a golden light, the colors of the world around her merging into a dreamlike blur.

She had known that this moment would come. The day she would set off on the path that had been set before her. But standing here, with the weight of the world pressing on her shoulders, she could hardly comprehend the magnitude of what she was about to do.

The temple, according to the map, was hidden deep within the heart of the forest, far from the prying eyes of the world. It was a place where time seemed to stand still, untouched by the passage of centuries. The legends spoke of its power, of the ancient secrets it guarded—secrets that could change the course of history itself. But what those secrets were, no one knew.

Meera's mind swirled with questions, doubts, and fears. What if she wasn't ready? What if the temple was nothing more than a myth, a story spun by the elders to keep curious souls at bay? But then she thought of the man, the quiet stranger who had guided her thus far. His calm confidence had given her strength when she needed it most. If he believed in her, then perhaps, just perhaps, she could do this.

The forest loomed ahead, its dark shadows and towering trees inviting her into the unknown. The path was narrow, almost hidden, and as she stepped onto it, she felt a strange sense of being watched. A thousand years of forgotten history seemed to echo in the air, the whispers of those who had walked this same path before her.

She took a deep breath, feeling the weight of her decision settling in. There was no turning back now. The temple was real. She had seen it in the map, felt its pull deep within her. But what awaited her there? Was it a treasure trove of ancient wisdom? Or a test of strength and courage beyond anything she had ever faced?

As the last rays of sunlight faded behind the trees, Meera pushed forward, her resolve hardening with each step. She wasn't sure what lay ahead, but she knew one thing for certain: she had to find the truth. She had to unlock the mysteries of the temple, no matter the cost.

Her thoughts were interrupted by a rustling sound in the bushes to her right. She froze, her heart skipping a beat. For a moment, the forest seemed to hold its breath. The rustling grew louder, closer, until a figure stepped out of the shadows.

A man, cloaked in dark robes, stood before her. His face was obscured by the hood of his cloak, but his eyes—piercing, intense—glinted in the dim light. For a moment, they stood there, staring at each other, neither speaking nor moving. The air between them crackled with an unspoken tension.

Meera's heart raced. Who was this man? Was he friend or foe? She took a step back, instinctively reaching for the dagger at her side. The man, however, made no move to approach her.

"You seek the temple," he said, his voice low and gravelly, as though it had been years since he had spoken. "But be warned, young one. It is not a place for the faint of heart. Many have come before you, seeking its power. But few have returned. And those who did..." He trailed off, his eyes darkening with some unspoken fear.

Meera didn't know how to respond. The stories, the warnings, everything had been vague. She had never expected to encounter anyone along the way, let alone someone who seemed to know exactly what she was after.

"Who are you?" she demanded, her voice steady despite the storm raging inside her.

The man's lips curled into a faint smile, though his eyes remained cold and unreadable. "I am the keeper of secrets," he replied cryptically. "And I have been waiting for you."

Before she could ask more, the man turned and began walking deeper into the forest, his footsteps silent against the ground. Meera hesitated for only a moment before following him. What choice did she have? He seemed to know more about the temple than she did, and if there was one thing Meera had learned on this journey, it was that she couldn't afford to ignore anyone who knew more than she did.

The journey had just begun. And with this mysterious figure by her side, she was about to discover things she never could have imagined.

The Path Unfolds

Meera followed the man through the dense undergrowth, each step she took feeling more uncertain than the last. The forest had changed since they entered. What had once been a welcoming space, filled with the scent of earth and the rustle of wind, now felt suffocating, almost alive in a way that made the hairs on the back of her neck stand on end. The trees loomed higher, their twisted branches creaking under the weight of ages. The air was heavy, and every whisper of wind felt like a warning.

The man ahead of her moved with the ease of someone who knew this forest well, his steps silent, and his cloak barely brushing the ground. Meera struggled to keep up, her every footfall muffled by the thick carpet of leaves beneath her boots. There was no moon tonight; only the faint glow of bioluminescent plants that dotted the forest floor illuminated their way.

Despite her fear, Meera couldn't shake the feeling that this was exactly where she was supposed to be. This was no ordinary journey. It wasn't about reaching the temple alone—it was about something deeper, something greater. The path she was on was more than just a physical road to a destination. It was a journey of the spirit, a test of her courage, her resolve, and her ability to uncover the truth.

"Do you know where we're going?" she asked, her voice barely a whisper as it was swallowed by the dense air.

The man didn't answer immediately. He continued walking, his pace unhurried. It wasn't until she almost caught up to him that he spoke.

"To the temple," he said simply. "Where else would we go?"

Meera furrowed her brow, trying to make sense of his words. Of course, they were headed to the temple—but something about his tone suggested there was more to it than that. She had been preparing for this journey her entire life, but now, with each step deeper into the forest, she felt as if she were entering an entirely different realm, one where the rules of her world no longer applied.

The trees began to thin out, revealing a clearing up ahead. Meera quickened her pace, eager to see what lay beyond. But as they neared the clearing, the air seemed to thicken even further. A low hum vibrated in the air, like a distant chant, resonating deep within her bones.

Suddenly, the man stopped. His hand raised to signal for silence. Meera froze.

Ahead, in the center of the clearing, a massive stone structure loomed in the distance, partially obscured by the thick mists that hovered just above the ground. It was the temple. The sight of it made Meera's breath catch in her throat. Its jagged edges and towering spires rose like a vision from another world, shrouded in mystery and ancient power.

But the sight of the temple also raised a question she had been avoiding asking herself since she began this journey: what exactly was she seeking? What lay within those stone walls, hidden from the world for so long? The truth? Or perhaps something much darker?

The man turned to her, his eyes narrowing as if reading her thoughts. "Not all answers are meant to be understood immediately," he said cryptically. "Some truths must be uncovered slowly, piece by piece. And you, Meera, have the strength to endure what is to come. That is why you are here."

Meera felt a chill run down her spine. She wasn't sure if his words were meant to comfort her or prepare her for what lay ahead, but they only deepened her sense of unease.

"Is it safe?" she asked, her voice trembling despite her best efforts to remain calm.

The man didn't respond, but his gaze seemed to say it all: the journey was about to get much more difficult.

As they moved forward, the hum grew louder, more insistent, and the ground beneath their feet began to vibrate with an almost imperceptible energy. The temple was alive, and it was waiting for her.

With each step, the darkness seemed to close in, the shadows stretching like fingers eager to grasp her. Meera's breath quickened, but she pressed on, determined to face whatever came next. This was her path—the path to uncover the secrets of the temple and her destiny.

The Silent Guardians

The temple loomed ahead like a forgotten sentinel, guarding its secrets with a silence that felt oppressive. As Meera and the man moved closer, the air around them thickened, each step taken in eerie stillness. The trees that once surrounded the temple cleared, revealing the full extent of the ancient structure. Its massive stone walls were covered with strange carvings—symbols she had never seen before, depicting creatures and deities in strange, otherworldly poses. The stone steps leading up to the entrance seemed to stretch endlessly upward, disappearing into the shadows of the temple's colossal arches.

Meera stopped at the base of the stairs, her heart pounding in her chest. The air felt heavier here, thick with history and mystery. She glanced at the man beside her, seeking reassurance, but his face remained unreadable, his expression as impassive as the stones that surrounded them.

"You must enter alone," the man said, his voice low, almost swallowed by the heavy atmosphere. "The temple will not let you pass unless you are ready to face its trials."

Meera's eyes widened. "What do you mean? Trials?"

"The temple tests those who seek its wisdom," he explained. "Only those who have the strength to endure will be allowed to uncover the truth hidden within."

Meera's hands trembled at her sides. She had been prepared for many things—danger, uncertainty, the weight of the journey—but she hadn't anticipated this. She had thought that once she reached the temple, answers would come easily, that the path would reveal itself in a clear, unbroken line. But now, standing before the massive stone structure, she understood that the temple was far more complex than she had ever imagined.

The man stepped back, his eyes darkening. "You will not be the same when you emerge from this place. But it is necessary. It is the only way."

Meera nodded, though a sense of unease washed over her. She had come here with a single purpose in mind: to uncover the truth. But now, that truth seemed more elusive than ever, tangled in the shadows that seemed to seep from the very stones of the temple.

Taking a deep breath, Meera stepped forward, her footsteps echoing against the cold stone of the temple's entrance. As she ascended the first few steps, the temperature dropped suddenly, and the air grew even heavier. It was as though the temple itself were breathing, exhaling ancient secrets into the night. Her mind raced with questions—what awaited her inside? What did the man mean by trials? And most importantly, would she be able to survive whatever challenges lay ahead?

At the top of the stairs, the massive wooden doors of the temple stood wide open, as if inviting her in. But as Meera approached, she noticed that the door wasn't opening of its own accord. There was a mechanism at work—a hidden force that had pushed the door open just enough for her to pass.

Stepping over the threshold, she found herself in the heart of the temple. The interior was as vast as it was dark, with towering pillars that seemed to stretch into infinity. Strange, glowing markings adorned the walls, casting an eerie light across the cavernous space. The ground beneath her feet was cold and smooth, as if polished by centuries of footsteps.

A low hum filled the air, the same resonance she had heard earlier, now stronger, almost vibrating with intensity. The sound seemed to emanate from deep within the temple, as if it were coming from the very heart of the structure itself.

Meera looked around, her senses on high alert. The air was thick with the scent of incense and something darker, something she couldn't quite identify. It was the smell of forgotten secrets, of things hidden away for too long.

As her eyes adjusted to the dim light, she saw movement in the shadows. Figures, tall and cloaked in robes, stood silently at the far corners of the temple, their eyes glowing faintly. They were the guardians. Meera had heard of such protectors—silent sentinels that watched over sacred spaces, waiting for intruders, ready to test those who dared to enter.

The figures didn't move as she approached, but she could feel their gaze upon her, as though they were studying her, evaluating her worth. One of the figures stepped forward, its face obscured by the hood of its robe. In its hand, it held a large, intricately carved staff, the top of which glowed with a faint, otherworldly light.

"State your purpose," the figure intoned, its voice deep and resonant, filling the vast space of the temple.

Meera stood still, her heart racing. This was the moment she had been waiting for—the moment when she would prove herself worthy of the truth hidden within these ancient walls. She took a deep breath, steadying herself, and answered.

"I seek the truth. I wish to uncover the knowledge that has been hidden for so long."

The figure nodded slowly, as if considering her words carefully. Then, without a word, it turned and motioned for her to follow.

The Trials of the Ancients

The cloaked figure led Meera deeper into the temple, past rows of ancient stone pillars that seemed to whisper secrets of a bygone era. The low hum continued to reverberate through the stone walls, growing louder and more intense the further they ventured. The temperature dropped even further, and the faint scent of incense mingled with something sharp, metallic, and unsettling.

The figure didn't speak, but Meera felt a growing sense of urgency. She had come here to uncover the truth, to find answers that would unlock the mysteries of her past, yet the silence around her felt oppressive, as though the very air held its breath, waiting for something to happen.

As they neared the heart of the temple, the shadows grew longer, more foreboding. The glowing markings on the walls intensified, their shapes shifting like living things.

The light cast by these symbols seemed to pulse, reacting to each step Meera took, as if the temple itself were alive, aware of her presence.

Finally, they reached a large chamber, its walls adorned with more glowing symbols, each one a different pattern, a different puzzle. At the center of the room stood a massive stone pedestal, its surface covered in intricate carvings. On top of the pedestal was a large, golden urn, its lid encrusted with gems that gleamed in the dim light.

Meera's heart skipped a beat. Though she had heard of the urn, she had never seen it before. It was said to hold the wisdom of the ancients, a knowledge so powerful that those who sought it had to prove themselves worthy.

The cloaked figure stopped in front of the pedestal and turned to Meera. For the first time, its glowing eyes met hers, and it spoke again.

"You seek the truth," it said, its voice deep and resonant. "But truth comes at a price. You must pass the trials to earn the knowledge you seek."

Meera's breath caught in her throat. Trials? She hadn't expected this. But she had come too far to turn back now. Her curiosity, her need to know, drove her forward.

"I'm ready," she said, her voice steady despite the apprehension building in her chest.

The figure raised its staff, and the ground beneath Meera's feet began to tremble. The air thickened, and a low, rumbling sound echoed through the chamber. The glowing symbols on the walls shifted, their shapes merging and separating like shifting constellations.

"Your first trial," the figure intoned, "is the trial of courage."

The air in the room seemed to contract, pressing in on her from all sides. Meera took a deep breath, trying to steady her racing heart. She could feel the presence of something, or someone, watching her. The darkness in the chamber seemed to deepen, and from the corner of her eye, she saw movement—something shifting in the shadows.

Suddenly, a dark shape lunged at her from the darkness, and Meera stumbled backwards, her heart leaping in her chest. But the shape was gone before she could fully react, swallowed by the shadows once more.

Another shape appeared, this time closer, its eyes glowing red in the dim light. Meera's pulse quickened, her body tense. She wanted to run, to escape, but her feet were rooted to the spot, as if the temple itself was holding her in place.

The figure at the pedestal raised its staff again, and the shadow disappeared.

"You must face your fears," it said, its voice echoing in the silence. "You are not alone in this place. The trials will test you in ways you cannot imagine. If you wish to uncover the truth, you must learn to stand firm in the face of fear."

Meera nodded, her heart still pounding. She had felt the fear, the primal instinct to flee, but she had stayed. She hadn't let it control her.

The figure turned away from her, motioning for her to approach the pedestal.

"Your second trial," it said, "is the trial of wisdom."

Meera stepped forward, her eyes fixed on the urn. The carvings on its surface seemed to come to life as she approached, the symbols shifting and rearranging before her eyes. There was a question hidden in the patterns, a riddle that she could not yet comprehend.

"You must answer the question," the figure intoned. "What is the true nature of wisdom?"

Meera stared at the symbols, her mind racing. Wisdom... what was wisdom? She had always thought of it as the ability to understand, to solve problems, to make the right decisions. But here, in this place, with the weight of centuries pressing down on her, she realized that wisdom was more than just knowledge.

She thought about the journey that had led her here, the lessons she had learned, and the people she had met. Wisdom was not just about knowing the right answers—it was about understanding the world around her, the choices she made, and the consequences of those choices.

"The true nature of wisdom," she said slowly, "is the ability to see beyond what is in front of you, to understand not just the world, but your place in it."

The figure's eyes glowed brighter for a moment, and then it nodded in approval.

"You have answered correctly," it said, its voice tinged with approval. "You are ready for the final trial."

Meera's heart raced again, though this time, it was not from fear. She was ready. She could feel it in her bones. She had faced her fear, she had understood the nature of wisdom, and now, she was ready to face whatever came next.

The Truth Revealed

The air was thick with anticipation as Meera stood in front of the ancient pedestal, her eyes fixed on the urn. The cloaked figure stood silently, waiting for her next move, its glowing eyes unreadable.

For a moment, Meera hesitated. The weight of the trials she had just faced pressed heavily on her mind. The shadows, the fear, the riddles—it all felt like too much. Yet, she knew there was no turning back. She had come this far, and the answers she sought were within her grasp.

"Are you ready?" the figure asked, its voice barely a whisper.

Meera nodded, her resolve hardening. "I'm ready."

The figure raised its staff one last time, and the symbols on the walls seemed to come alive, swirling around her in a chaotic dance. The light from the glowing markings intensified, casting long shadows that seemed to stretch across the chamber. The hum of energy that had surrounded her from the moment she entered the temple became deafening.

The urn on the pedestal began to glow with an otherworldly light, its surface shimmering as though it were made of liquid gold. The air crackled with power, and Meera could feel her heart racing, a mix of excitement and fear flooding her senses.

The figure stepped aside, allowing Meera to approach the pedestal. She took a deep breath, the weight of the moment settling over her like a heavy cloak. As her fingers touched the urn, a surge of energy shot through her, and the world seemed to shift. The walls of the temple vanished, replaced by visions of ancient times—times that felt both distant and familiar.

She saw a woman, cloaked in the same mysterious garb as the figure standing beside her. The woman was in the heart of a bustling city, surrounded by the beauty of nature and the noise of everyday life. She saw people laughing, working, living their lives, all in harmony with the world around them.

Then, the vision shifted. The city was no longer vibrant, but instead, it was in ruins. People were scattered, running in all directions, as a great darkness consumed everything in its path. The woman stood at the center, her eyes glowing with the same light that had filled the temple. She reached out, trying to stop the darkness, but it was futile. The city fell, and with it, the woman.

The vision faded, and Meera was left standing in the temple once more, her heart racing, her breath shallow. She looked at the figure, its eyes still glowing brightly.

"What was that?" she asked, her voice trembling.

"That," the figure replied, "was the past. The woman you saw was a guardian of the temple, someone who sought to protect the truth. She failed, but her legacy lives on. And now, it is your turn."

Meera's mind spun with the weight of the vision. The woman, the city, the darkness—what did it all mean? And how was it connected to her?

"You have passed the trials, Meera," the figure said, its voice soft. "You have faced your fears, you have learned the nature of wisdom, and now you are ready for the truth. The urn holds the answers you seek. But the truth is not always what we expect. Sometimes, it is more painful than we can bear."

Meera stepped back from the pedestal, her mind reeling. She had come to the temple seeking answers, but what she had found only raised more questions.

"Take the urn," the figure continued. "It is yours now. The truth is yours to uncover, but remember, knowledge comes with a price. Are you willing to pay it?"

Meera hesitated, her hand hovering over the urn. The weight of the decision pressed on her, and she felt the full weight of her journey. She had faced the trials, had stood up to the fear, and had unlocked the wisdom she needed. But this... this was different. This was the moment that would define everything.

Finally, with a deep breath, Meera closed her eyes and reached out. Her fingers brushed the surface of the urn, and the moment they made contact, a surge of energy filled her body. She felt her heart racing, her mind flooding with visions, with knowledge. The truth, the answers she had sought for so long, were now before her. But they were not clear, simple answers. They were tangled, layered with mysteries and secrets she could barely begin to understand.

As the vision faded, she pulled her hand away from the urn, her breath coming in sharp gasps. The figure before her watched silently, its expression unreadable.

"You have chosen, Meera," the figure said. "The journey does not end here. The truth you have uncovered will guide you, but remember—what you have learned comes with a responsibility. Use it wisely."

Meera nodded, the weight of the urn still in her hands. She didn't know where her journey would take her next, but she knew one thing for sure: she was ready for whatever came next.

With the urn in hand, she turned to leave the temple, the truth now a part of her, forever entwined with her destiny.

Chapter 3

Unraveling Secrets

The Silent Witness

The city streets hummed with the usual noise—the rush of cars, the chime of distant church bells, and the occasional shout of vendors peddling their wares. Yet, in the midst of the chaos, there was a silence. A quiet stillness had settled in the heart of Rohan's mind.

For the first time since his investigation began, he was beginning to feel a shift in the air. A sense of foreboding, something he couldn't quite explain. The case had been straightforward at first—missing persons, strange disappearances, and hints of darker forces at play. But now, as he walked the same streets where the victims once had been, it felt as if the walls were watching him, or rather, he was being watched.

Rohan paused at the corner of a narrow alley, his instincts alert. He glanced up at the old brick buildings, their windows like eyes staring down at him. Something was off. He could feel it. The shadows seemed to stretch longer today, as if they knew more than they let on. Every step felt heavier.

He had been here before, but this time was different. This wasn't just another case. The usual suspects—the usual culprits of dark alleys and forgotten corners—had faded into the background. There was something deeper, something more insidious lying beneath.

Rohan's eyes narrowed as he surveyed the alley ahead. The shadows twisted unnaturally, and the once familiar streetlights now seemed to flicker ominously. The air grew colder, as if it were holding its breath, waiting for something to happen.

His fingers brushed against the cold, rusted railing of the alleyway. It was here that he had received the first tip-off—a cryptic message left on his phone: "*Follow the witness, or all is lost.*"

The words echoed in his mind like a distant whisper: *Follow the witness.* But who was this witness? And why had they remained silent for so long?

Rohan's grip tightened on the railing as a sudden noise broke his thoughts. There was a soft shuffle from behind. His heart raced as he turned swiftly, his instincts honed from years of working in the dark underbelly of the city. But there was nothing—just the empty alley, its grimy walls standing like silent sentinels.

His breath came out in a sharp exhale. He was being paranoid, he thought. It was just his mind playing tricks on him. After all, who would be watching him? Who could possibly have known what he was doing?

But deep inside, he couldn't shake the feeling that he wasn't alone.

Suddenly, a figure emerged from the shadows. Not a person, but a cat—a sleek, black cat with glowing yellow eyes. It crossed the alley with such grace that for a brief moment, Rohan wondered if he had seen a ghost.

The cat paused for a moment, looking directly at Rohan before vanishing into the darkness. Its eyes glowed briefly, like two small lanterns in the dark. A shiver ran down his spine. Was it a sign? Or was it just another trick of the night?

That was it—the sign, the silent witness.

Rohan's thoughts churned. The cat wasn't just an ordinary stray. It felt purposeful, as though it had been waiting for him. Its gaze had been almost knowing. *What are you trying to tell me?* he muttered under his breath, before taking off down the alley, his heart pounding in his chest. He had to find this witness—this elusive source of the cryptic message.

As he turned the corner, a single thought remained fixed in his mind: The shadows were speaking to him. And he was listening.

Whispers in the Dark

Rohan's steps quickened as he walked further down the alley, the sense of being watched growing stronger with each passing second. The city, with its sprawling chaos, felt so far away now. Here, in the dim light of the broken street lamps, the world seemed smaller, quieter, more menacing.

The shadows danced around him, as if alive, bending and stretching with the breeze. His heart thudded in his chest as the alley narrowed, walls closing in. His hand instinctively reached for the cold metal of his gun, tucked securely beneath his jacket. But he knew it wasn't the weapon he would need. It was his wits, his instincts, and his ability to read the signs.

There were no sounds now—no cars, no voices—just the echo of his footsteps. And then, there it was—a low, barely audible whisper. It wasn't coming from behind him, nor was it coming from the street. It was coming from above, from the fire escape overhead.

Rohan froze, his breath catching in his throat. The whisper repeated, soft, insistent. "He's coming for you."

A shiver ran down his spine. He looked up, but all he saw were the rusted, winding stairs of the fire escape, leading into the darkness above. No one was there. At least, no one he could see.

Was it the cat again? The strange feline with the glowing eyes? Rohan wasn't sure. But one thing was certain: whoever or whatever was speaking to him had been waiting, watching. And it wasn't going to let him go.

His mind raced back to the cryptic message he had received earlier: "*Follow the witness, or all is lost.*" What did it mean? Who was the witness? And why did it feel like the very walls were closing in on him?

Rohan's senses were on high alert. He scanned the surroundings, eyes darting between the darkened windows and the empty street. Then, as if on cue, a figure appeared. It was a shadow, moving with purpose across the street at the far end of the alley, too quick, too deliberate.

Without thinking, Rohan bolted forward, his legs pumping with adrenaline. He needed answers. Whoever this was or whatever this was, he would find out.

But as he rounded the corner, the figure vanished. Gone, like smoke in the night.

Rohan stood frozen, his chest heaving with heavy breaths. His mind screamed, "This is not a coincidence." The whispers were getting louder, and now, they were speaking directly to him. He had been led here to this very moment.

The alley was silent again. The air was thick with the scent of damp concrete. And there it was—the cat, once again. Its glowing yellow eyes pierced the darkness as it sat calmly in the center of the alley, its gaze fixed on Rohan.

He hesitated for a moment, and then took a step forward, drawn toward the creature as if by an invisible force. The cat didn't move, didn't flinch. It just stared at him. A soft, guttural purr resonated from deep within its chest, sending a chill down Rohan's spine.

Then, as quickly as it had appeared, the cat turned and sprinted down the alley, disappearing into the shadows.

Rohan stood there for a moment, bewildered. Every fiber of his being screamed that this was no ordinary cat. This was no stray. This was part of something much larger—something far more dangerous than he could have imagined.

He glanced at his phone—no messages, no calls. No one had seen him go down this alley except the cat and the whispers.

The silence was now deafening. The whispers had stopped, but the sense of dread remained. Rohan knew one thing for sure now: someone or something was playing with him. And it was only just beginning.

The Mysterious Call

Rohan leaned against the brick wall, his mind still whirling from the unsettling events in the alley. The cat, the whispers, the figure that vanished without a trace—everything felt like it was spiraling into a darkness he couldn't escape.

His phone buzzed in his pocket. He pulled it out instinctively, as if his entire being was waiting for this moment. The screen lit up with an unknown number, the digits unfamiliar and foreign. A tightness gripped his chest.

He answered on the second ring.

There was no greeting, no voice, only silence.

His heart pounded in his ears as he strained to hear anything, anything at all. Then, just as he was about to hang up, a voice broke through the stillness.

"Rohan, you're closer than you think. Don't trust the shadows. They will deceive you."

The voice was smooth, almost like velvet, but there was something chilling about it—a coldness in the words that made Rohan's skin crawl. It sounded familiar, yet distant, like a voice he had once heard in his dreams.

"Who is this?" Rohan demanded, his voice hoarse, betraying his growing anxiety. "What do you want?"

A soft chuckle echoed from the other end of the line, sending a wave of unease through Rohan. "You don't need to know who I am, Rohan. Not yet. But you will. Trust me."

Before he could respond, the line went dead. The call disconnected abruptly, leaving Rohan standing there, the phone still pressed to his ear, his pulse racing.

He stared at the screen for a long moment, trying to comprehend what had just happened. His thoughts were tangled, his mind screaming for answers he couldn't find. Who was the person on the other end? And what did they mean by "the shadows will deceive you"?

Rohan's grip tightened around the phone. It wasn't just a prank. This was deliberate. It was a message, a warning. But from whom? And why?

The unsettling feeling from earlier still lingered, like a dark cloud hanging over him. He needed to make sense of it all, but where to start?

His eyes scanned the alley, then the street beyond. It was quiet now, too quiet. The world felt oddly still, as if holding its breath, waiting for something to happen.

Suddenly, he felt a cold chill crawl up his spine. He wasn't alone.

Rohan turned sharply, his eyes darting around the surroundings. There was no one. But that eerie feeling, that sense of being watched, was undeniable. His instincts were screaming at him to leave, but his feet remained planted firmly on the ground.

His phone buzzed again.

This time, Rohan didn't hesitate. He pulled it out, his fingers trembling slightly. The message was brief: "*The cat knows more than you think.*"

Rohan frowned, his heart skipping a beat. The cat—the strange creature from earlier—was it somehow involved in all this? Was it the one watching him?

Before he could think further, a shadow passed overhead, fleeting and quick, as though it were simply an illusion. But Rohan didn't believe in coincidences anymore. He knew this was no accident. Something, or someone, was leading him down this twisted path, step by step.

And the worst part was that he didn't know who was pulling the strings.

With a heavy heart and a mind filled with unanswered questions, Rohan began walking again, this time with more purpose. The night was still, but the air felt charged, like electricity crackling just beneath the surface. The game was on. And he was no longer just a player. He was a pawn.

But who was the real master behind the scenes?

The Vanishing Act

Rohan had barely taken a few steps before the world around him seemed to shift. The streets were quieter now, eerily so. The distant hum of traffic and the usual clamor of the city had faded into an unsettling silence. It was as if the city itself had gone to sleep, leaving him to navigate a labyrinth of his own fears and uncertainties.

His mind raced with questions, each one feeding into the next like a never-ending loop. Who was that voice on the phone? What did it mean by *the shadows will deceive you*"? And the cat—what was its connection to all of this?

As he turned the corner onto a narrow side street, a strange sense of déjà vu washed over him. The air felt thicker here, as though it held secrets of its own. He could almost feel something watching him, like invisible eyes were observing his every move. The hairs on the back of his neck stood up.

His phone buzzed again, shattering the stillness of his thoughts. Without thinking, he grabbed it. A new message appeared, this time from an unknown contact: *"Don't trust the mirrors, Rohan. They never show the whole picture."*

A cold shiver ran down his spine. It was a cryptic warning, one that added another layer of confusion to the puzzle he was desperately trying to piece together. He had no idea who was sending him these messages, but the sense of urgency and the strange, almost personal nature of the words made him feel as if he were being pulled deeper into a web of deceit and lies.

He reached into his jacket pocket, pulling out a crumpled piece of paper. It was the same one he had found earlier, the one with the cryptic symbols on it. His fingers traced the strange markings as he tried to make sense of them, but they were as elusive as the shadows he had been warned about.

Suddenly, the ground beneath his feet seemed to shift, and he stumbled. Looking up, he found himself standing in front of an old, decrepit building. The windows were dark, and the door hung slightly ajar, as if inviting him in.

Rohan froze. This place felt wrong. There was something off about it, like it had been waiting for him, biding its time.

Without thinking, he stepped forward, drawn to the door as if by some invisible force. His breath came faster now, and his heart raced in his chest. This was it—he had found it—the next clue—the next piece of the puzzle.

The door creaked open slowly, revealing a darkened hallway. The air inside was stale, thick with the smell of dust and decay. It was as if the building had been abandoned for years, yet the faint sense of life still lingered.

Rohan stepped inside, his footsteps muffled by the worn, creaky floorboards beneath him. He could feel the weight of the silence pressing down on him, the darkness enveloping him like a heavy cloak.

He moved cautiously down the hallway, his senses on high alert. The place felt like a tomb, as though it had been waiting for someone to uncover its secrets. But what was he supposed to find here? What could possibly be hidden in this forgotten place?

As he walked deeper into the building, his phone buzzed again. Another message: *"Look behind you, Rohan. You are being followed."*

His heart skipped a beat. He spun around, his breath catching in his throat. There, in the shadows at the end of the hallway, he saw it—a figure.

It was just a silhouette, barely visible in the dim light, but Rohan could feel its presence. And he knew, without a doubt, that it was no coincidence. The figure was following him. It was waiting for him to make the next move.

Rohan took a deep breath, steadying himself. He had come too far to turn back now.

With a final glance at the figure, he continued forward, deeper into the darkness. He had to find out what was happening, and no shadow, no mystery, was going to stop him.

The Truth Revealed

Rohan's heartbeat echoed in his ears as he continued down the dark hallway. Every step felt heavier, as though the air around him was thickening with every breath he took. The figure, or rather the shadow, still loomed in the distance, always just out of reach but never far enough to escape his vision.

His mind raced. Every part of him screamed to turn back, to leave this place, but something held him there. He couldn't stop now—not after everything that had led him here. The phone messages, the cryptic symbols, the strange encounters—it was all pointing to this very moment.

The figure in the hallway shifted slightly, and for a moment, Rohan thought he saw something in its eyes. It was a glimmer of recognition, perhaps? Or was it just a trick of the light? Whatever it was, it made him pause for a second.

As he stepped forward again, the silence became almost unbearable. Each creak of the floor under his feet seemed to magnify in the stillness, as if every sound was being amplified a thousand times. He was being watched. He could feel it.

The hallway seemed to stretch before him, endless in its dark expanse. Every corner he turned, every door he passed, only led him further into the unknown. He had no idea what awaited him, only that it was something he needed to face.

The phone buzzed again: *"It's all connected, Rohan. The shadows, the symbols, the cat. Everything you've seen is leading you here. Do you see it yet?"*

He felt a cold shiver run down his spine. The message felt too personal, too direct. Who was behind this? Who was orchestrating this twisted game?

Rohan's fingers tightened around the phone, his grip growing firm. As if driven by a new wave of clarity, he took a deep breath and pressed forward. He had to know. He had to see it through to the end.

Ahead, the hallway forked. Two paths stretched before him, each disappearing into darkness.

The shadow seemed to drift towards the right, as though beckoning him to follow.

Without hesitation, Rohan took the right path.

The further he walked, the colder the air became, and the darker the hallway seemed to grow. It was as though the very walls were closing in on him. And then, at the end of the corridor, he saw a faint light.

It flickered, like a dying flame, casting erratic shadows against the walls.

He quickened his pace, the sounds of his footsteps growing louder as he neared the light. It was coming from an old wooden door that stood slightly ajar.

A figure stood in the doorway, half hidden in the darkness, but Rohan could see enough. The person had their back to him, but he could tell it was no ordinary figure.

It was a woman.

A woman he recognized.

"Meera?" Rohan whispered, barely daring to believe what his eyes were telling him.

The woman turned slowly, and her eyes met his. Her expression was unreadable, but there was something in her gaze—a mixture of sadness, fear, and a strange sense of calm, as if she had known this moment was coming.

"Meera, what is all of this?" Rohan asked, his voice trembling.

She didn't answer right away. Instead, she stepped back, motioning for him to enter.

Rohan hesitated, unsure of what he was about to walk into, but his feet moved on their own. He stepped through the doorway, and the room was suddenly filled with light, a stark contrast to the darkness of the hallway.

The room was simple, but it was clear that it had once been something more. On the walls were old photographs, many of them faded and torn, with unfamiliar faces staring back at him. But one photo caught his eye.

It was a picture of a cat, perched on a windowsill, staring directly at the camera.

Suddenly, everything clicked. The cat, the messages, the strange dreams—it was all connected. It had all led him here.

And the truth, Rohan realized, was right in front of him.

Meera walked to a small desk in the corner of the room and picked up a journal. She handed it to Rohan with a quiet sigh.

"It's time for you to know the truth," she said softly.

He opened the journal, and what he read made his blood run cold.

The truth was darker than he could have imagined. It wasn't just a game. It wasn't some twisted riddle. This had been part of a larger plan—a conspiracy that stretched far beyond anything Rohan could have ever fathomed.

Meera's voice broke through his thoughts.

"I never wanted you to find out like this," she said, her eyes filled with sorrow. "But now that you know, there's no turning back."

Rohan looked up from the journal, his mind reeling. "What do you mean? What is this all about?"

Meera's eyes softened. "You've been chosen, Rohan—chosen to uncover the truth. The world isn't what you think it is. The shadows, they're not just shadows. And the cat, it's not just a cat."

Rohan's breath caught in his throat. "Then what is it?"

Meera smiled faintly, though there was no joy in it. "The answer's been staring you in the face this entire time. The shadows have always been a part of us. And now, you must make a choice."

Chapter 4

The Final Reckoning

The Heart of Darkness

Rohan stood at the precipice, the truth unfolding in his mind like a carefully orchestrated symphony. But it wasn't the music he had expected. No, it was a darker, more sinister tune—a melody that had been playing in the background of his life without him ever realizing it. Now, he could hear it clearly, each note reverberating with purpose.

He had come to understand that the shadows were not just a metaphor. They weren't just figments of his imagination. They were real, tangible forces that had been influencing every part of his life. The cat, the strange messages, the dreams—it was all part of a much larger design.

The journal in his hands was heavier than it had been moments ago. Each page seemed to hold the weight of the world, filled with secrets he wasn't sure he was ready to uncover. But he had no choice. This was his path now, and there was no turning back.

Meera stood beside him, her presence calm yet somehow distant. Her eyes, filled with knowledge Rohan couldn't even begin to comprehend, met his. She spoke in a quiet voice, yet it carried authority.

"You've been chosen for this, Rohan. There's no escaping it."

He turned toward her, his mind spinning with a thousand questions. "Chosen? For what? What does all of this mean?"

Her gaze softened, but there was no sympathy in her eyes. "It means you are the one who will break the cycle. The shadows, the symbols, the game—it's all a test—a test to see if you are worthy."

"Worthy of what?" Rohan asked, his voice rising with frustration.

"Worthy of uncovering the truth, and worthy of stopping what's coming," Meera replied, her tone steady. "But the truth comes at a cost. It always does."

The room seemed to grow colder as her words hung in the air. The weight of her statement settled over Rohan like a thick fog, clouding his thoughts.

He had always believed that knowledge was power. But now, standing on the edge of this dark revelation, he wasn't so sure. What good was power if it led to more darkness? What good was truth if it was something he couldn't even begin to understand?

Meera seemed to sense his hesitation. "You're scared, aren't you?"

Rohan didn't answer, but the truth hung in the air like a thousand unspoken words.

"Fear is natural," Meera continued, "but it's not what will guide you. It's the choices you make now that will decide everything."

"Choices..." Rohan murmured. "How am I supposed to make a choice when I don't even know what the consequences are?"

Meera's expression remained unreadable, but there was a flicker of something in her eyes—an understanding that Rohan couldn't quite grasp. "That's the test. The unknown is what will shape you. The choice is yours, and yours alone."

He looked down at the journal again, the pages filled with cryptic symbols and references to ancient texts. This wasn't just about him anymore. This was about something much larger. The truth was something that could either save the world or tear it apart. And Rohan had to decide which side he would be on.

The Path of Choices

Rohan's mind whirled as the weight of Meera's words sank in. He had always believed that every choice was his own, a simple decision between right and wrong, black and white. But now, standing in the midst of these ancient truths, he felt that everything he thought he knew was slipping away. There was no clear-cut line between good and evil anymore—only shades of gray, twisting into something much more complex than he could have ever imagined.

The journal seemed to pulse in his hands, as though alive, its pages filled with cryptic symbols that now felt like a language he should have known all along. But he couldn't make sense of them—not yet. There was a key, though, somewhere hidden in these words—a key that would unlock not only the truth of his destiny but also the power to change the course of everything.

Meera's voice broke through his thoughts. "The time is almost upon us, Rohan. The path ahead is filled with darkness. You'll need to decide whether to face it or let it consume you."

He looked at her, his eyes filled with questions, but she said nothing more. Instead, she turned, her face set with determination. She knew something he didn't—something that he had to uncover on his own.

Rohan walked toward the desk, his fingers grazing over the journal. The faint glow of the lantern flickered, casting long shadows across the room. The words within the journal seemed to shift before his eyes, rearranging themselves into patterns that he could almost understand. Almost.

There was a code in these pages—an ancient language that, when deciphered, would guide him to the truth. But how could he decipher it? What was the key that would unlock the mystery?

The symbols danced in front of his eyes, mocking him with their complexity. Yet, a sudden thought flashed in his mind—a memory, one from long ago. A childhood game he used to play with his sister, where they would write notes in a secret language, just the two of them. Could it be that simple? Could the key to this puzzle be something as innocent as a game?

A flicker of understanding ignited in his mind. Maybe it wasn't about overthinking the symbols or their meanings. Maybe it was about the feeling they evoked, the way they seemed to resonate with something deep inside him. He had to trust his instincts, his gut. The answers were already there. He just needed to reach out and grasp them.

Suddenly, the room grew colder, and Rohan shivered as the shadows seemed to lengthen. He could hear a faint whisper, a voice calling his name from the dark corners of the room. The hairs on the back of his neck stood up. Was it his imagination, or was someone or something watching him?

Before he could react, the journal in his hands began to glow. A soft, ethereal light seeped from the pages, illuminating the symbols in front of him. The whispers grew louder, more urgent. His heart raced, and he felt an overwhelming urge to follow the path that the journal was showing him.

Without thinking, Rohan opened the journal to a page he hadn't noticed before. The ink on this page was fresh, as if it had been written just for him. The words were simple, yet profound: *"The choice is yours, Rohan. Will you face the darkness and uncover the truth, or will you turn away and let it claim you?"*

Rohan's breath caught in his throat. This wasn't just about him anymore. This was about the world—about the future. He could feel the weight of his decision pressing down on him, the consequences of each choice already unfolding before his eyes.

With trembling hands, he closed the journal and stood up, looking at Meera, who had been watching him silently the entire time. Her gaze was unwavering, as though she knew exactly what was going through his mind.

"You have to decide, Rohan," she said quietly. "The darkness is coming. And only you can stop it."

The Crossroads of Fate

Rohan stood at the edge of the precipice, his mind in turmoil. The journal, now closed, lay heavy in his hands as if it weighed down on his very soul. The secrets it held were not easily digested, but the truth had been revealed, and there was no denying the power it possessed.

Meera's words echoed in his mind: *"The choice is yours, Rohan. What will you do with the truth now that you have it?"*

What would he do?

The truth felt like an anchor, something that could either pull him to the depths or set him free. But what was the cost of freedom? Was it too high to pay? He thought back to the people whose lives had been torn apart by the very forces he was now chasing—his own past, his own mistakes, his own choices. The weight of those choices pressed on him like a chain, and yet he couldn't bring himself to look away from the path before him.

As if on cue, a cold gust of wind swept through the room, rustling the pages of the journal in his hands. A chill ran down his spine. The whispers had returned—those whispers that he had heard in the dark corners of his mind, the voices that had always guided him to this moment. But they weren't comforting. They were sharp and insistent, like a broken record that kept repeating the same phrase over and over again: *"It's not over. The game has just begun."*

Rohan's breath hitched. His pulse quickened. He could feel the presence of something or someone watching him from the shadows. His body tensed, and instinctively, he reached for the gun at his side. But it wasn't the gun that would save him now. It was his mind, his resolve.

The shadows seemed to stretch, curling and twisting around him as though they were alive, reacting to his every movement. The air grew thicker, more oppressive, and the weight of the journal in his hands felt heavier with each passing second. He was at a crossroads. He had uncovered the truth, but with it came the knowledge that the fight wasn't over. It had only just begun.

"Do you truly believe you can stop it, Rohan?" a voice whispered from the darkness.

Rohan spun around, heart racing. There, standing in the doorway, was a figure. It was tall, cloaked in darkness, its face hidden in the shadows. He couldn't make out its features, but he knew, deep down, that this was no coincidence. This figure was part of the puzzle—part of the game.

"You don't understand," Rohan said, his voice trembling despite himself. "This isn't just a game. People's lives are at stake. This is real."

The figure took a slow step forward, the sound of its boots echoing in the silence. "Is it, Rohan? Is it real? Or is it just another layer of deception?"

Rohan's grip tightened around the journal. "You're wrong. I know what I've seen. I know what's at stake."

The figure paused, its form a blur in the dim light. "The truth is a dangerous thing to possess. Once it's revealed, there's no turning back. You'll never be the same."

Rohan swallowed hard. He knew the figure was right. There was no going back. His choices, his actions, would forever shape the course of what was to come. He had crossed the line. And now, he had to face the consequences.

The figure stepped into the light, its face still obscured. "You've been chosen, Rohan. You didn't have a choice in that. But now, you must decide how the story ends."

Rohan's pulse quickened. The weight of the moment pressed down on him. The figure was right. This was the final reckoning. The game was no longer something he could walk away from. It had consumed him.

The journal, the whispers, the shadows—it was all leading to this.

Rohan took a deep breath. "I won't run anymore."

The figure nodded, a slight, almost imperceptible smile forming on its lips. "Then it begins."

The Veil Lifts

Rohan's heart pounded as the figure in front of him stepped back into the shadows. The tension in the air was thick, almost suffocating. Every fiber of his being screamed at him to run, to escape this moment. But he couldn't. He had crossed this line, and there was no going back.

"You can't hide forever, Rohan," the figure's voice echoed from the dark corners of the room. *"The truth will find you, whether you're ready or not."*

The words sliced through him like a knife. The figure was right. Rohan had spent his life running—first from the haunting ghosts of his past, and then from the secrets he uncovered. But there was no more running now. The truth was here, and it was demanding his attention.

He stood frozen in place, his mind whirling with the enormity of the decision he was about to make. The weight of the journal in his hands grew heavier with each passing moment. The secrets it contained were no longer just ink on paper. They were real. They were alive.

With a sudden clarity, Rohan realized that the figure had given him something far more valuable than answers. It had given him the choice—the choice to face the truth, or to let it consume him.

As the figure moved silently through the shadows, Rohan could almost feel its eyes watching him, studying him. *"What are you waiting for?"* the voice whispered from the darkness.

Rohan clenched his jaw. He wasn't waiting anymore. He was ready—ready to face whatever came next.

He stepped forward, holding the journal tightly against his chest. The room felt colder, darker, the walls closing in on him. Every creak of the floorboards beneath his feet seemed to echo in the stillness, each sound amplifying his sense of foreboding.

Then, in the far corner of the room, he saw it—the figure, now visible in the light. It was a woman. Her face was partially obscured by the shadows, but her eyes glowed with an otherworldly intensity. She seemed almost ethereal, like she didn't belong in this world.

Her gaze met his, and Rohan felt a jolt in his chest. There was something familiar about her, something he couldn't quite place. A faint memory tugged at the edges of his consciousness, but it remained just out of reach.

"Who are you?" Rohan demanded, his voice shaking despite his efforts to remain steady.

The woman stepped closer, the shadows swirling around her like a cloak. "I am the one who's been watching," she said softly, her voice like silk, but cold as ice. "I am the one who's been waiting for you to make this choice."

Rohan's breath caught in his throat. The words hit him like a ton of bricks. *Watching? Waiting?* Had she been the one behind the whispers? The cryptic messages? Was she the one who had led him here?

"You knew," he whispered, realization dawning on him. "You knew what I would find. You knew what the journal would reveal."

The woman smiled, though it wasn't a comforting smile. It was more of a knowing, distant smile, as though she were watching a play unfold that she had already seen a thousand times before. "I didn't know. I only knew that you had to make the choice. We all do."

Rohan felt the weight of her words. This wasn't just about him anymore. This was about something bigger—something that stretched far beyond his understanding.

The woman extended her hand toward him, her fingers slender and graceful. "You've come this far, Rohan. But now, you must decide. Will you accept the truth and face the darkness? Or will you turn away, and let it claim you?"

The room seemed to tilt, the weight of her words pulling him deeper into the abyss. He glanced down at the journal in his hands, the pages fluttering as if urging him to make a choice. But what was the right choice? Could he even know?

Rohan swallowed hard. The truth had never been so clear—and yet so elusive. He could feel the darkness at the edges of his vision, could hear the whispers calling him, pulling him toward something he wasn't sure he was ready for. But one thing was certain: if he didn't act now, if he didn't choose to face it, the darkness would swallow him whole.

With a deep breath, Rohan took the woman's hand.

"I'm ready," he said, his voice steady. "Let the truth be revealed."

The Choice of Shadows

Rohan's fingers tightened around the woman's hand, feeling the coldness seep into his skin. It was as if the very shadows were reaching through her, into him, pulling him deeper into a world he hadn't been prepared to enter. The room around them seemed to shift, the walls closing in, the air thickening with every passing second. His pulse raced in his chest, the sound deafening in his ears.

The woman's eyes were calm, yet her presence was suffused with an eerie calmness that made him feel like a pawn in a game he didn't fully understand.

"You have made your choice, Rohan," she said, her voice soft but unwavering. "Now, you must live with the consequences."

Rohan's mind raced. *Consequences*. He had known all along that the path he had chosen would lead him to a point of no return. He had crossed the line. The truth was before him, but the cost was yet to be seen.

He glanced down at the journal in his hands. It had been his guide, his map, his constant companion through this twisted maze. Now, it felt heavier than ever.

The woman released her grip on his hand, her face unreadable. She stepped back, merging into the shadows once more. "The truth will be revealed. But know this, Rohan: the shadows never go away. They only change their shape. And they will always be waiting for you."

Her words reverberated in his mind. He had spent his entire life running from the shadows, but now they were a part of him. There was no escaping them, no matter how hard he tried.

Rohan stood still for a moment, letting the weight of her words settle into his bones. But then, he took a deep breath, his gaze fixed on the journal. This was his moment—the culmination of everything he had endured, everything he had fought for.

The journal's pages fluttered once again, as though urging him to take the final step. With trembling hands, Rohan opened it. This time, the symbols were different. The cryptic patterns that had tormented him seemed to shift, rearranging themselves into something far more legible. The message was clear: *"The shadows will guide you, but only you can choose which path to take. Will you embrace the light, or will you surrender to the darkness?"*

Rohan's breath caught in his throat. The light and darkness had always been separate in his mind—two opposing forces. But now, in the face of this revelation, he understood that the truth wasn't about choosing one over the other. It was about balance, about acknowledging both sides of the coin and finding a way to navigate through them.

He closed the journal slowly, his hand trembling as he set it down on the table beside him. There was no need for it anymore. The answers had always been inside him, buried beneath layers of fear and doubt. Now, he could see them clearly.

The room around him seemed to fade away, and for a moment, all that remained was the feeling of something shifting inside him. The shadows no longer felt like enemies. They were a part of him—his past, his mistakes, his choices. But they didn't have to define him.

Rohan took one last look at the empty space where the woman had been. She was gone, but her presence lingered, a reminder of the decision he had made. The world outside the walls of the temple awaited him, and it was a world that would never be the same.

He stepped out of the shadows, leaving the past behind. The journey had been long and painful, but it had led him here—to this moment, to this choice.

And as he walked away from the temple, Rohan knew that the truth he had uncovered wasn't just about the shadows. It was about him. It was about choosing to embrace both the light and the darkness, to find peace in the chaos.

The game was over.

But the story was just beginning.